W9-AYN-229

Ajay Navaria | Unclaimed Terrain

Ajay Navaria

GIRAMONDO

Unclaimed Terrain

Published 2015
from the Writing & Society Research Centre
at the University of Western Sydney
by the Giramondo Publishing Company
PO Box 752 Artarmon NSW 1570 Australia
www.giramondopublishing.com

© Hindi originals, Ajay Navaria
© English translation, Laura Brueck
First published in India by Navayana Publishing 2013

Designed by Harry Williamson
Typeset by Andrew Davies
in 10/14.5 pt Minion Pro
Printed and bound by Ligare Book Printers
Distributed in Australia by NewSouth Books

National Library of Australia
Cataloguing-in-Publication data:
Navaria, Ajay, author.
Unclaimed Terrain / Ajay Navaria.
ISBN: 9781922146892 (paperback)

891.433

All rights reserved. No part of this publication may be
reproduced, stored in a retrieval system or transmitted in any
form or by any means electronic, mechanical, photocopying or
otherwise without the prior permission of the publisher.

Translated from the Hindi by Laura Brueck
With an Introduction by S. Anand

To the characters in my stories
who fight for their dreams of justice,
and to the tradition that teaches us
to struggle for dignity, equality, and freedom

Contents

Contents

Introduction

Ajay Navaria makes the untouchable-dalit the everyman of his stories.

I could start by describing Ajay Navaria as a dalit writer. But that seems limiting and unfair. After all, brahmin and other privileged-caste writers from the subcontinent, when translated or when their work travels to new areas, do not wear their caste identity as a prefix. They appear to be just writers, hence universal (even if classified as Third World, postcolonial or Indian). But in almost all Indian languages, Hindi in this case, a reader infers the caste of a writer from his very name: everyone knows that 'Munshi' Premchand (1880–1936), born Dhanpat Rai Srivastav, considered the greatest modern Hindi writer, belonged to the caste of accountants and scribes, kayasths, ranked just below the brahmin; Shrilal Shukla (1925–2011), best known for his satirical novel **Raag Darbari**, *bears a brahmin surname; the name of the recently deceased Rajendra Yadav (1929–2013), who revived* **Hans**, *the premier literary magazine founded by Premchand, announces his middle-caste shudra identity; the fine contemporary Hindi poet Ashok Vajpeyi (b. 1941) reveals that he is a brahmin as he introduces himself. Even those who hide behind pseudonyms are easily found out. This is how it works in rural India and, with some variations, in metropolitan India. And so it does in the world of arts and letters.*

Suffice to say, every name emits a radioactive signal called caste. Every name is a parade of imagined history; the announcement of privilege or the lack of it. There are four broad categories called **varna** *in the hereditary caste system – brahmins (priests), kshatriyas (soldiers), vaishyas (traders) and shudras (servants). The outcast untouchables, about thirty million people, comprising close to twenty five percent of the total Indian population (if we include the untouchables who embraced Christianity and Islam), fall outside the pale of the fourfold varna system and were meant to be slaves with duties only and no rights whatsoever.*

What Bhimrao Ramji Ambedkar said in his 1936 tract **Annihilation of Caste***, 'turn in any direction you like, caste is the monster that crosses your path', remains true to this day. Ambedkar, born in 1891 into an untouchable mahar family in western India, not too far from the 'Gateway of India' in Bombay that adorns the cover of this edition, was a civil rights leader like no other. Imagine the anger of Malcolm X fused with the erudition of W.E.B. Dubois (with whom Ambedkar corresponded) and laced with the pragmatism of John Dewey (with whom he studied at Columbia University in 1913–16). Ambedkar – the architect of an enlightened, secular Constitution he superimposed on an unenlightened caste-obsessed society – is a hero to Ajay Navaria and to the enlightened dalit men who figure in the stories here. A few months before his death, in 1956, Ambedkar formally renounced Hinduism and embraced an anti-metaphysical Buddhism along with half a million followers. Today, enlightened dalits continue such liberation struggles in new ways.*

Caste's graded hierarchy, in Ambedkar's words, is 'an ascending scale of reverence and a descending scale of contempt' in which there is 'no scope for the growth of sentiments of equality and fraternity.' Across India, there are close to 2,500 endogamous castes known as **jātis**, *many of them specific to certain regions. New castes are formed with almost every generation. It's like the Raktabija – 'the demon-king who spawned demons in his own image at every drop spilt of his blood' – in Navaria's story 'Tattoo'. The adivasis, an umbrella term for all India's indigenous inhabitants, fall outside the caste system's shadow (though they are recruited by right-wing ideologues into being 'Hindu').*

Anyone who reads Ajay Navaria in Hindi knows of him as a dalit writer. Since the time when many of these stories were published in Hindi, first in literary journals and then in collections, Navaria has been outspoken about being dalit. He has been associated with the Dalit Lekhak Sangh (Dalit Writers Association, formed in 1999), and in 2014 became its president. The situation, for Navaria, is more or less like being an assertive black writer in the US of the 1960s – a James Baldwin-like figure. Some dalits are skeptical about him, as are writers born into privileged castes – especially when Navaria creates protagonists like the one in 'The Scream', who, sodomised and brutalised by his caste overlords, lands in Bombay and soon becomes a hugely sought-after masseur-gigolo. The unnamed dalit man becomes 'Tyson' and uses his enormous penis as his business card. His very profession demands that he breaks caste rules every day.

Navaria's dalit characters are capable of pettiness and hate, confusion and uncertainty; his non-dalits are capable of love, there's hope for them. They are human because they are flawed. They are all flawed because they are human. In his world, humanity is the flaw that redeems you. Nobody is etched in black and white – everyone is forever becoming something. Navaria's strength is also that he's among the few dalit writers who imaginatively and empathetically portray non-dalit characters; he inhabits what he has not experienced. This is remarkable given that so far it is only privileged non-dalits of elite castes who have arrogated to themselves the task of writing about lives of which they have had little understanding or experience. In a world where dalits still have limited access to, say, brahmin lives, Navaria bravely claims an unclaimed terrain.

In the preface of his first short story collection **Patkatha Aur Anya Kahaniyan** (The Script and Other Stories) published in Hindi in 2006, Navaria ponders this. 'It is no coincidence that the main characters or the dreaming protagonists of these stories are dalit. In today's society, it is inevitable that dalits are confronted by non-dalits at every step and every moment. Consequently it is very difficult for them to keep intact their self-respect and identity (**asmita**). After entering this labyrinth, dalits often forget the way out. Lost in this labyrinth they either try to become like non-dalits or it is expected of them to live and function according to the norms and standards set by non-dalits. How has the story been different in literature?'

With Navaria's fiction you enter the world of the urban, Hindi-speaking *dalit male with rural, small-town roots telling you what it is to live in a city like Delhi or Bombay. Here, you will come across a panoply of caste names whose significance cannot be translated or even explained; they do not unravel themselves in English. These names reveal possibilities and foreclosures; they invoke punishments and privileges around which everyday social life in India revolves.*

Each of the modern, dalit male characters in Navaria's world carries a little of Ambedkar in him; they embrace names that reveal pride, honour and dignity – even when the assertion, or the mere expression, of these hard-won aspects of identity can make one lose them. In the Maupassant-like story 'New Custom', the term **darbar** *functions like 'master', an honorific suffix used for a regal kshatriya-figure. And given the manner in which the unnamed protagonist conducts himself, he appears to be a darbar to the roadside vendor of chai. A suave well-dressed dalit person can easily pass for being someone he or she is not supposed to be. Caste is often not inscribed on one's skin. It thus becomes more intractable – it has to be observed and sometimes inferred slowly. An average Hindu, for whom caste is paramount, will start playing detective in almost every social situation. Class, and the attendant material benefits it bestows ('refined' speech, the clothes you wear, your intellectual vocation, the food you eat), can erase the stigma of untouchability – at least temporarily, as in the story 'Subcontinent', where Siddharth Nirmal, the dalit, can employ a 'Garhwali brahmin driver, Bhatt'. But Navaria lets neither his characters* nor his readers arrive at easy conclusions. What he builds in one story, he demolishes in another. In 'Tattoo' we witness the anxieties and struggles of a middle-aged, gym-going bureaucrat who initially introduces himself simply as Subhash Kumar, dropping his Paswan surname since that would disclose his untouchable identity. While he's mostly worried that people may catch sight of his unbranded worn-out shoes, it is the tattoo on his right forearm that looms large. Identity has been literally branded on his consciousness and being, whether he wears branded shoes or not.

Let us see how names work in another seemingly simple story, 'Yes Sir'. 'Tiwari! Some water!' is how this story begins. To a reader in Northern India, Tiwari immediately signifies a brahmin. And the person giving him orders is Narottam Saroj, the manager. Such a name, unlike Ramnarayan Tiwari's, does not easily give away caste. It's a little puzzle with a whiff of defiant Buddhism. In fact, it sends out a strong anticaste signal. Narottam in Hindi means a man ('nar') who is great ('uttam'); Saroj stands for lotus, the symbol of enlightenment, the lotus posture of Buddha. As we soon discover, the bearer of this name is a dalit-untouchable, being served chai and water by a brahmin peon who has to run errands for his social inferior. Tiwari feels this is what happens in **kaliyug**, the Dark Age that is the present, when ideas of equality and justice rock the divinely sanctioned order (brahmins on top, untouchables at the bottom). How Navaria handles this complete role reversal, a reversal made possible by the policy of reservation or the system of 'quota' (as affirmative action is called in India), forms the basis of this story. A petty 'dimwitted' Tiwari brahmin is made to appear grateful, even indebted, to his dalit boss. But that some kind of hierarchy has to remain – where someone orders, someone serves – is an emphasis given by Navaria.

Names are all too important in Navaria's world. In the opening story 'Sacrifice', the dalit male narrator Avinash (which means indestructible, a name he gives himself after rejecting his birth-name, Ramesar), mocks old-fashioned names that invoke fealty to Hindu gods and goddesses. He shouts down his orthodox father who does not care much for Ambedkar and the Buddhist modernity he's supposed to herald: 'I will name my children Abraham or Siddharth, but not Ramlal or Shyamlal.' In this story we also find that the upwardly mobile yet 'backward' shudra castes, such as meenas and gujjars, are behaving like thakurs – a landed, powerful caste – and now torment dalits. In 'New Custom', it is the other way round: it is the father who warns the son about returning to the village – 'Be careful, everything is just as it was there'.

Premchand is a spectre that looms large over the world of modern Hindi literature. He was someone who keenly put his faith in Gandhi and in the anticolonial actions that have come to be recounted in textbooks and the public discourse as the 'freedom struggle'. Premchand produced a huge corpus of fiction: 12 novels and some 250 short stories. Many of his fictions feature dalits, sometimes as protagonists – in stories such as 'Kafan' (The Shroud), 'Doodh ka daam' (The Price of Milk), 'Thakur ka kuan' (The Thakur's Well) and 'Sadgati' (Deliverance). This was at a time when dalits were not subjectivities portrayed in literature but used casually as fringe characters. Some of these stories and novels have been taught over the decades in high-school and university syllabuses and many of them have been turned into plays, television series and feature films (in 1981, Satyajit Ray made a film called **Sadgati**). These stories and their canonisation, in turn, shape the perception of caste for those who receive a modern education. What is the problem with Premchand and his mode of so-called realistic writing? Premchand had a distinct distaste for Ambedkar's politics of liberation and justice. He believed in 'Mahatma' Gandhi's politics of piety that included a patronising renaming of untouchables as 'harijan' – children of god, an appellation rejected by dalits. After sighting the 'Mahatma' in 1919, Premchand wrote: 'A glimpse of Gandhiji wrought such a miracle that a half-dead man like myself got a new lease of life.'

Gandhi and Ambedkar clashed in the 1930s over the question of what the fate of untouchables and the caste system would be once the British left India. Ambedkar, and the radical anti-caste tradition he came to represent, believed that liberal institutions established by the British, like courts, schools, the railways, hospitals – where everyone irrespective of social origins was to be treated as equal in principle – had blunted the deleterious effects of the caste system. Ambedkar sought certain rights *and safeguards for untouchables, who were despised and abhorred not just by Hindus but by the elites amongst Muslims and Christians too. He sought to have these guarantees in place before the British left the subcontinent, for he feared that when power was transferred to the Nehru–Gandhi-led Indian National Congress party, it would merely mean a return to the rule of brahmins and other elite castes. Gandhi opposed Ambedkar's claim to speak on behalf of untouchables; Gandhi, who came to believe in his own sainthood, argued that he could speak for everyone since he spoke for 'the nation'.*

Dalits were crushed between Premchand, often termed the 'Father of Modern Hindi Literature', and Gandhi, who enjoys the status of the 'Father of the Nation'. Most dalit writers today reject both these father figures: patricide becomes a necessary rite of passage. In effect, Premchand chose the cry 'Mahatma Gandhi ki Jai' (Victory to Gandhi the Great) while enlightened dalits rallied around Ambedkar with 'Jai Bhim' – sometimes a greeting, sometimes a war cry that shortens Ambedkar's first name, Bhimrao, making 'Jai Bhim!' a kind of Black Power Salute.

This account of Premchand's significance is necessary because one of Navaria's key stories has Premchand and Ambedkar appearing together. What inspired this? In 2004–5, on the occasion of the 125th anniversary of Premchand's birth, some dalit writers argued that universities should stop teaching his stories, because they reinforce caste stereotypes. For instance, Madhav and Ghisu are such drunkards in the story 'Kafan' (The Shroud) that they spend the money they raise for buying a shroud for the dead daughter-in-law on booze instead. Whatever Premchand's intentions, limitations, and literary merits, some dalits demanded 'cuts' (edits) in his work or argued that it should not be taught at all; some even made a bonfire of his books. Navaria, and many writers who also happened to be dalit, did not favour such revisionism. Navaria's response was an act of brazen literary heist: 'Uttar Katha', a response story, that figures as 'Hello Premchand' in this volume, features a slew of characters who appear in many of Premchand's fictions. Navaria here not only imagines Ambedkar and Premchand having a conversation, he uses half a dozen characters and situations from Premchand's 'dalit stories' and writes his concerns onto and into them. Mangal, Ghisu, Madhav, Devidin, Halku – these dalit characters reappear from Premchand's oeuvre. In Navaria's world they form an Ambedkarite community based on fraternity and solidarity; they are not mere orphans crushed by fate or the weight of caste – after all, **dalit** etymologically means 'crushed' or 'broken down' in Pali and Sanskrit.

In Premchand's 1934 story, 'Doodh ka daam' (The Price of Milk), Mangal the scavenger-caste boy loses his mother and is forced, like her, to shovel the shit of his caste superiors in exchange for leftover food as his wage; his sole companion is a stray dog. Premchand is indeed heavy-handed in trapping this character in hapless abjection. In Navaria's 'Hello Premchand', we have the orphaned Mangal being helped, not only by other dalits of the village, but also by a progressive Sevanand 'Arya' who drops his caste surname Yadav in reformist zeal. At Sevanand's house, Mangal encounters the autobiographies of established dalit writers, such as Omprakash Valmiki's **Joothan**, Surajpal Chauhan's **Tiraskrit**, and Roop Narayan Sonkar's **Nagphani**. Importantly, Mangal, whom Premchand abandoned to his caste-determined fate, returns to the village in Navaria's story as Collector Mangal Das, an officer of the elite Indian Administrative Service. And he is not acrimonious or embittered.

S. Anand

Sacrifice

'Mehhhh!' Behind the heart-rending scream, a deep, bone-chilling voice commanded, 'Press the legs down hard, Kalu.' Piloo struggled, prostrate on the ground. I held him down with all my strength. He still trembled as he lay there but no longer made a sound. Yet his eyes remained fixed on mine as though he were asking how I could so betray our friendship. Having slit his throat, Kaka, my father, sat calmly sharpening his knife. I wanted to run away, but it was too late. I, seven years old, holding down the feet of a seven-month-old goat I had fed and raised…running away would only have meant another of Kaka's vigorous beatings. To be born weak is a mistake, but to remain weak is a crime. Despite these big words, I was indeed weak then, my friend. The kid was lying there, completely at peace. Now and then his body would spasm, and I would break into a sweat. My eyes would well up. Several minutes later, Piloo became completely still.

'Well, get up now!' Kaka had finished sharpening his knife and had returned to the shade of the neem tree where Piloo's body lay. I was still holding his legs down tight.

'Let go now. You think he's going to get up and run? Go tie the rope to the neem.'

I got up mechanically and tied the rope to a strong branch. His throat was slit, and the blood that poured from his neck had already filled a brass pot. Kaka hoisted up the corpse, and in one fell swoop separated Piloo's head from his body.

'Go give it to your Jiji, she'll make natar from it,' said Kaka casually, motioning toward the pot full of blood.

I knew my mother would put the blood on the stove, add oil, chilli, salt, and onion, and cook the natar. Then everyone would eat it with relish, as they always did. Kaka cut Piloo's legs off at the knees and separated the trotters. Setting these aside with the head, Kaka used the fat tendons from Piloo's haunches to tie him upside down from the neem's branch. Drops of blood were still oozing from the corpse. Kaka was engrossed in slowly skinning the goat from the knees with a practiced hand.

'Come here, watch how we remove the hide. It shouldn't tear, else it'll go for cheap. And there shouldn't be any flesh sticking to it either. Watch carefully! Where's your attention?'

I had given the pot of blood to Jiji for the natar. Seeing me standing at a distance, Kaka shouted at me. I slunk closer to him. My beloved child, Piloo, hanging upside down – it was a terrifying sight. Kaka had flayed his hide. In just a short while, my gamboling, playful Piloo had been reduced to a pile of meat. Soon customers would buy his flesh from the shop. Someone would buy his testicles, someone his head, and someone else his trotters. Some poor tanner's wife would buy his entrails to satisfy her alcoholic husband's desire and to fill her hungry children's stomachs. No one would remember my bounding Piloo, my sweet kid.

Such would have been my thoughts at that moment.

'Idiot! Are you watching or not? Are you paying attention? Here, grab this!' Kaka peeled off the skin like he was taking off a sweater. He turned his knife to Piloo's belly next and slit it. Piloo's intestines dangled like a bag. Having separated the intestines, kidneys, liver, and lungs, Kaka clutched them in his hands. 'Goddamn buyers! What can I do? Everyone wants tender kid's meat,' I heard him mutter.

The sun had started to slide westward. A humid heat was spreading. The shadow of Piloo hanging from the tree had grown longer. Kaka squatted nearby and quietly puffed on a bidi. He looked like a vulture. But my mind was on Piloo. Mewing, leaping, bounding…my Piloo! I'd looked after him ever since Saroo, our nanny goat, birthed him. He was my only friend, he was my brother. I used to feed him leaves from my hand. I would seat him in my lap, and we'd play the whole afternoon.

I'd gone along with Kaka when he got Saroo mated. Saroo gave two kids. Piloo was a billy and Shanti a nanny. When Kaka was butchering Piloo, Saroo had come and stood at a distance. She kept bleating. But Piloo wasn't watching Saroo. His gaze was fixed on me. Perhaps he was watching his butcher's son become a butcher himself. Saroo gave no milk for two days. What else could she do? It's the weaker species' lot to end up on the plates of the stronger, brother. Kaka slung Piloo across his cycle and left for the market. He fastened the head and trotters to the cycle basket and hung the torso on the handlebars. As was his habit, he called out to Jiji when he set out. Piloo was so pink on the inside – the way flesh is after it has been washed repeatedly. When I saw him for the last time, dangling from the cycle, it seemed to me he was twitching.

Kaka had left, and I threw up as soon as he was gone. I collapsed on the cot under the neem tree. I don't know when I fell asleep. Piloo came to me in my dream. He was snarling like a tiger. He had big, sharp fangs. Kaka and I knelt before him. He was coming straight for us, with sharp knives in his hands. I saw Kaka turn into a goat. 'Jiji!' I screamed. My eyes tore open, but Jiji wasn't there. Darkness hadn't deepened yet. It was still twilight. But night would gather soon enough.

Jiji returned. Seeing me lying on the cot, she put a hand on my forehead.

'Oh, you're burning up. Come on, get up and lie down inside.' She spoke lovingly.

'Where did you go?' I asked tearfully.

'To the well to fetch some water,' she said, trying to lift me into her arms. Jiji laid me down inside and brought mustard seeds and chillies to drive away the evil eye. This is how mothers are. If the slightest misfortune befalls one of their own, they'll go to any lengths – take the loved one to a saint, an ascetic, an exorcist, or a country doctor.

When darkness enveloped the thatched hut, Jiji lit a small lamp. Kaka had come back from the market.

'Hey Kalu, bring some salt! Where are you, Kalu's ma, can't you hear me?' Kaka's voice thundered through the house as he came in, just like it did every day. He'd have already pulled out a half-bottle of Gulab-brand country liquor from a fold of his dhoti, poured it into a cup, and had a few swigs. Lying inside, listening to his voice, I could guess what would happen in the next few moments. This was Kaka's daily ritual. He couldn't go to sleep without downing a half-bottle of Gulab or Kasturi. He would be so impatient to drink that even waiting for salt felt like a lifetime.

'I told you not to do this. He's only a little boy – but you just have to have your own way! He's burning up. He didn't even eat the natar.' This was Jiji. She had joined Kaka outside the hut.

'What happened?' Kaka's tone was softer now.

'He was crying. Kaka killed even Piloo, he kept saying,' said Jiji.

'So he thinks we should have raised him up to be a buck? What's the point? He would have been butchered anyway. You know customers snap up kid meat quicker. What can you do about people? No one asks for older meat when they can get a kid's. I kept a little by – here, cook it.' Kaka must have then unwrapped the meat from his shoulder-towel and given it to Jiji, like he always did. The cloth would be blood-soaked. I imagined all this as I lay there.

'Don't tell Kalu, just tell him it's some other meat,' I heard Kaka say.

'This is my story, son. You asked me to tell it, so I did. I was just Khusman's age then. This is why I said to get Khusman out of here. But Bhai Saheb insisted that this sacrifice was for the boy's sake and that I should cut it right in front of him. I didn't say anything. But the boy got scared. Seeing meat already cut up is one thing, brother, and watching a goat being butchered is quite another. I wasn't born a butcher. It took Kaka's training and beatings to make me one.' Kalu glanced at the door behind which he'd seen Kushan leave. Kalu's eyes – lacklustre and still – were suffused with dejection. Wrenching his eyes away, he now looked at me. But his mind was elsewhere. Like someone trying to pick food stuck in his teeth, eyes fixed at one place, mind somewhere else.

His pain ran deep – tied to a post from which it could neither break free nor keep still. And today was the day of the sacrifice to thank the gods for a son, for which Father had specially called Kalu from the village. How could I convince Father that the power of making babies lay in my thighs and my wife's calves, and was not the result of some divine intervention? Anyway, Kalu was here, and Father had promised him the hide and 251 rupees, besides the cost of travel. Owing to his abiding faith, Father had acquired the habit of adding a token one rupee to any amount. And these days you didn't find a spare rupee so easily. Kalu was a famed butcher in his neighbourhood, Father had told us. He also said Kalu would take one look at his watch and set himself to make mincemeat in five minutes, the pieces still quivering. 'He'd cut the pieces so clean! Can boys today cut like that? They don't have such skill. Fashion! That's all that interests them. These days, the meat you get has so much scrap stuck to it. But your mouth waters at the very sight of Kalu's mincemeat.' And as Father spoke, he swallowed, salivating as though the mincemeat were already in his mouth.

I had stayed far away from this rite from the very beginning. I hadn't even left my room until Anita came in with Kushan. It was only then that I found out what had happened. I started charging out of the room in anger, but Anita stopped me: 'Wait! Avinash, let it go. It will just lead to pointless quarrel. Papa won't have much to say to you; it's me he'll taunt – me and my caste. He's just waiting for the opportunity. Let it go. It's only a few months more now, and we'll get the government flat. Jeering at me about my caste, he has...' Then she went quiet.

A while later, I emerged from the room. Father was sitting right outside the door. 'So, you've found the time to come out and join us? We work ourselves to the bone for you while you sit in the house like a big lord? This one's our first-born, Brother Kalu. Such shame he's brought on our caste, sneaking off and getting himself married to the daughter of some Gautam Buddha from Uttar Pradesh...he might as well have sliced my nose off. But I have such a big heart that I still made place for them in my home. Or they'd have been left without shelter,' said Father to Kalu, gesturing toward me. 'Arrey, at least greet Kalu,

Ramesar! He's like your uncle, say 'Ram-Ram'! If you've forgotten even this...what is it you people say? Yes, your 'Jai Bhim'!'

Ma's love overshadowed Father's behaviour. Otherwise Anita and I wouldn't have stayed there a single moment. Ma couldn't make Father understand, though. There wasn't a person in the world who could. He believed and would often proclaim that there wasn't anyone in the world as wise as he or as big a fool as I. And Ma? Ma loved Anita as much as she loved me. A mother is a mother – there isn't anyone in the world whose love can rival hers. She wasn't Anita's mother-in-law. She had made Anita her own, like a daughter.

I greeted Uncle Kalu and took a chair. Father sat in a chair opposite. Only Kalu was squatting on the floor, smoking a bidi. 'Why don't you sit up here?' I motioned toward an empty seat.

'No, no, brother, I'm fine here,' Kalu said, smiling. Seeing Kushan throw up had taken him back forty years. He'd already completed his work, filling the large pot with meat.

'Go get him, son,' Kalu said. Noticing the ooze encrusted in the corners of Kalu's kohl-lined eyes, I was faintly disgusted.

'Who?' I asked, tearing my eyes away from the filth in his eyes.

'What is that English-sounding name you gave your son, brother? I can't get my tongue around it. Khus...nam,' he said, stammering, and I laughed.

'Not Khusnam, Kushan.'

Embarrassed, he said, 'Yes, brother, Khusnan, Khusnan.'

'Arrey, who's going to remember, when you give him a name like that?' It was Father's turn to strike. As he walked toward us, he caught Kalu's words. I had been feeling relieved, thinking that he was leaving.

'It's all her doing. He's a hen-peck...' I glared at Father, and he was quiet for a moment. But he couldn't stay so for long.

'Should I be afraid of anyone in my own house? Since what I'm saying is true, I'll trumpet it out loud. Whoever doesn't like it can leave. Isn't that right, Kalu? He's under the spell of that black-haired woman. Aachaarji says that you go to heaven if you die in your own religion. I named the child Ramkumar, didn't I, brother? But no, he doesn't want to see us happy. The idiot says it stinks of slavery. He has a problem even with the name Ram! He changed his own name too. My younger one, Ramsahay – now he's a real man. He's such an obedient boy! And his wife wouldn't dare utter a word. If he raises his voice, she'll piss herself. I've given Ramsahay's son the name Ganeshi. Ganeshimal. When he grows up, this boy, Ganeshimal, will run the store.'

Father had started his usual litany of my shortcomings. I wanted at first to get up and leave, but I also still wanted to talk to Kalu. What we wish for, however, does not ever fully come our way; some undesired scraps somehow end up clinging to them. I was used to such crude talk. At the shop, however, he was a different Father altogether – sweet and soft-spoken. But when he closed the shop, he downed shutters on that Father as well. When talking to Ma, he took special pleasure in calling her relatives motherfucker, sisterfucker, cunt-spawned. Exchanging even a few civil words with Ma was a waste of breath for him.

'Brother Kalu, he has disgraced the goddess of our community. He has shamed me to boot. The matchmaker found him a match with a family in Jaipur. You know everything. What do we lack? But if the girl's family wants to give a dowry, why should we refuse? Everyone gives their daughter a good send-off. The matchmaker said the cash payment alone would come to five hundred thousand. But, brother, it's his damned luck – he showed up with this teacher woman. Now he'll get his wife to work, and he'll live off her earnings! She could work her whole life, and still not lay eyes on five hundred thousand. And if I'm still alive, I'd love to see what sort of people will marry his kids. God knows where he dredged her up from…'

'Shut up! Just shut up! Have you no shame?' I screamed so loudly that for a moment everyone was stunned. I knew that he was about to start insulting Anita's caste. I exploded, 'You've eaten us alive! Caste, caste, caste…what are we – dogs and cats? Who I married, who I shouldn't have…this is my business. You just harp on about the same thing over and over. I don't want to stay here at all. And please get it through your skull that I will name my children Abraham or Siddharth, but not Ramlal or Shyamlal. Do you get it?'

I had erupted. There's a limit to tolerance. Father knows that I stay quiet for Ma's sake, so he blabbers on. I've learned over the years that only screaming at him would shut him up. Now he sat in calm repose. In his white kurta-pyjama he looked just like a hypocrite heron, devout in its quiescence but merely waiting for its prey. I wanted to tell him that if it weren't for Dr Ambedkar, he would be sitting today in the butchers' quarter of some village, cutting up a goat. And his Ramsahay would be squatting by him, holding down the goat's feet. But in my anger I forgot to say all this.

Kalu, witnessing this domestic quarrel, had started quietly sharpening his knife. A few minutes later, Father got up and went inside. I forced a smile after he left. Seeing me smile, Kalu looked at me wide-eyed.

'Arrey, Uncle, such squabbles are a daily occurrence here. How long can I bottle all this up in my heart? This is the only way to make him stop. I feel bad speaking like this, but this is the only cure for him. Whoever yells louder than him, wins. Ma, Mama, Nana – he's gotten into the habit of yelling at all of them to make himself important, and these poor souls take it.' As I said this, I picked up a big, glistening knife lying near my chair. 'This is the truth about us, Uncle.' I drew the knife back and forth through the air.

'No, son, Bhai Saheb wasn't always like this. He was actually very cheerful and good-natured once. He lived in the village until he was about twenty; he came to Delhi only later, after his marriage. He left his wife behind in the village and came to the city for work. He had a thriving business. He sent a lot of money home; everyone there would talk about him. Five or six years after moving to Delhi, there was a fire, and all his goods burned to ashes. When he started over, your Dadaji told him to take his wife along, but Bhai Saheb kept putting it off with one excuse or another. Perhaps his wife hadn't found a place in his heart.' He smiled and lit another bidi. He blew on the matchstick several times to extinguish it.

'Sure! They got a free servant, my grandparents, so why would they insist?'

'No, no, brother, it was something else altogether. A big secret. Swear you won't reveal it ever, and I'll tell you.' His voice sank to an undertone.

'Alright, forget about it. Tell me, after you got a fever, did your father stop making you watch him butchering?' I brought the subject back to what I really wanted to talk about. Some people have a bad habit of backbiting.

'Arrey, when did Kaka ever relent so easily? He was very strict. He scold my Jiji a lot. He used to say, 'If you don't do the work of our ancestors, you think you'll become a government official and work in land records? There's dignity only in doing the work of your caste.' The fever went down in a couple of days. I used to go to the village school.

When I came home, I'd leave with Kaka for the market. There was only me. Jiji didn't have any other children. Even though Jiji tried to dissuade Kaka from taking me along, he wouldn't agree. In four or five years, I learned to butcher expertly. By the time I was thirteen, I could already butcher a few animals all by myself. People would tell Kaka, 'Your Kalya will make a great butcher one day!' Hearing this, Kaka's chest would swell with pride. This was just what he'd wanted. That I'd be his cane in his old age. Like Kaka, I too got into the habit of smoking a bidi when I was done butchering. Slowly, I got addicted to them too. Kaka caught me smoking many times but never scolded me.' Kalu picked up the knife and ran his thumb along the blade.

'So you never really studied?' I asked, and he started as though he'd been asleep.

'Well...I went to school till fourth grade, but after that I didn't really feel like it. The teachers' behaviour used to bug me. The brahmin and baniya kids teased me about my caste too. My heart would break. How long could I put up with daily humiliation? Then there was the market, where everyone praised my skill. So I quit my studies.' So many furrows on his brow. His heart was embittered by these harsh memories.

'But, Uncle, have you never felt bad about this bloodstained life? I mean – don't you think it is a sin to kill?' I had so many questions only he could answer.

'What sin, brother? Well, yes, in the beginning, it did feel wrong – for a couple of years. But then it became a habit. And people praised me. This boosted my morale. Brother, this is work. It's honest work, and its earnings are well deserved.' He spoke in a very restrained voice, as though he didn't really believe what he was saying.

I kept pushing him. 'Yes Uncle, it is work, but people think it's dirty, don't they? You were just saying that the brahmin and baniya kids, and the schoolteachers didn't treat you well. Didn't all of it happen because of this work?'

Suddenly he burst out angrily, 'Brother, if this work is dirty, then why don't people treat their thakur landlords as untouchable? Thakurs also hunt, eat meat. They even eat wild boar, deer, and rabbit. We butcher to fill our stomachs, but they…does anyone treat them as untouchable? No, no, the problem isn't with the profession, it's poverty. They treat us as untouchable because we're poor. Brahmins and baniyas wouldn't dare act insolent to the thakurs. Now the times are changing. Even meenas and gujjars have become thakurs. And now they've made it hard for us to live in the village.'

His logic was rustic yet irrefutable. I was forced to stop and think a few moments.

'I don't have any complaint about the work, but butchering a kid still breaks my heart,' the words suddenly flared out of him like a spark as he lit his bidi.

'So, Uncle, who else is in your family?' I asked, hoping for the conversation to take a more personal turn. He was quiet a moment, then replied, 'I had a wife. She left me about seven years ago.' His voice was heavy.

'Any children?' I asked, and the pain deepened in his eyes. He was quiet and said nothing further. I didn't ask again. Sometimes questions only aggravate grief, they do nothing to lend solace. I looked at my watch. It was 5:30. Night was gathering. These were the coldest days of January in Delhi.

'Khusnan must be asleep?' There was such tenderness in his voice that my heart flooded with warmth.

'Should I wake him?' I asked.

'No, let him sleep. If he sleeps, he'll forget, and that will be a good thing. What is your wife's name?' He asked in the same intimate tone.

'Anita,' was my short answer.

'And this means her family...' he pressed me further, and I understood that he too wanted to know her caste, so I stayed silent. But he didn't. People from the village are known for their directness.

'What is her caste, brother? Is she from our religion or...'

'Yes, she's from our caste. She's SC,' I cut him off bitterly. But the next moment, I regained my composure, and wondered why I always got so worked up when the matter of caste arose.

'Scheduled Caste means she is indeed low-born,' he said and

started to pull on his bidi quietly. I was nonplussed. He had no trouble accepting that he was low caste himself. The crime of gross ignorance...My mind spun, reeling into a vortex. I couldn't say a word for a while.

'Where are you lost, son? Did I anger you, asking about her caste?' he asked dejectedly.

'Yes. Drop it, Uncle.' I came back to the present.

'Her name also started with an A,' he said, smiling. I assumed he was talking about his wife or child.

'Whose?' I asked.

'The one your father loved,' he said with a wink. The moment he winked, he started to cough convulsively. The coughs turned into a fit, making his eyes bulge. I immediately filled a glass of water and brought it to him. He poured the water from the glass into his cupped palm and drank. He found some relief. When he finished, he ran a hooked forefinger through his grizzled moustache, gathering the water that clung to the hairs and flicking the drops aside. Watching him, I felt a kind of revulsion, but my eagerness to hear what he had to say only grew.

'Can even Father have been in love with someone? Which means someone could have loved him too? I don't believe it, Uncle!' I was amazed, also wondering how this man could say all this to me. But as he began to tell me more, there was no limit to my astonishment when I heard he was thirteen or fourteen years younger than Father, and just ten or so years older than me. He seemed so aged that I would never have imagined him much separated from Father in years.

'Arrey, brother, you wouldn't believe how deep their love was. Neither midday sun nor moonless night could stop them. Bhai Saheb got me to deliver a lot of love notes. They were completely wrapped up in each other. I was young, but I understood everything. This kind of knowledge comes quickly.' He winked his left eye again. As soon as he winked, he burst out coughing. There was a broad smile on his face. And a strange peace. Perhaps it was the calm of revealing a secret.

'What was her name?' I asked hesitantly. The excitement of getting to know this aspect of Father made my hair stand on end.

'Archana. She was brahmin.' As is done in villages, he mentioned her caste along with her name and winked his left eye again, which I found vulgar.

'Then?' I asked, 'Then what?'

'They were so much in love. She went to school and was in the highest class. Bhai Saheb used to graze his goats near the school in the hot afternoon sun. She often stepped out into the schoolyard under the pretext of drinking water. Brother, neither sun nor rain deters lovers. She was the headmaster's daughter. I have rarely seen such a good man. The headmaster didn't practice untouchability. One day he even sat me on his lap. His daughter was just like him. She was so fair, milk would have felt jealous. She had hands as soft as a five-day-old goat.

'One day Bhai Saheb gave me a letter. I approached her during school recess. She was by the big water pot, drinking from it. I was thirsty and said I wanted to drink too. She poured the water, but it all flowed out of my tiny hands. So she took both my hands and made a deep well of my joined palms, and told me that was how to do it. Then I took the letter from a fold of my dhoti and gave it to her. She quickly hid it in her blouse. Her hands were so soft. She was very beautiful. There wasn't anyone else as beautiful in the whole village. My Bhai Saheb was one in a million too.' He gazed intently at me. Then, lost in thought, dangling his arms on his knees, he drummed his fingers on the floor. He shifted his position like a clucking hen, and then sat motionless as though he'd been sitting that way for years.

Father was such a romantic! How could a man like that turn so heartless? Was this Father's revenge? Against himself, against others, against Ma?

'What was written in the letter? Did you read it?' I asked, trying to appear calm.

'How would I have known to read then? I was in first or second grade. But I had another boy read it on the sly,' he said, and my stomach fluttered.

'What did it say?'

'A handful of things. There was a poem. And then it said to meet in the evening at the base of the slope behind the temple.' He smiled, and I didn't like the smile.

'You must have gone too,' I said, and he became coy.

'Brother, I'd have been daft to let such an opportunity slip. My friend and I quietly crept under the cover of a tree and watched the two of them tussle.' He opened another packet of bidis; I urged him not to smoke when he had such a bad cough, and he returned the packet to his pocket. He was still squatting on the floor.

How long had I been watching him sit in this position? I wondered if this posture was something he had perfected. He must not have felt any pain from sitting like that. I would not be able to squat like him for two minutes; my feet would fall asleep and my legs would start to tingle.

'Why, were they fighting about something?' I feigned ignorance. It would have been better had I stayed quiet. But now that I'd spoken, it couldn't be taken back. Before Kalu could answer, Father appeared with a pair of tongs, carefully carrying a burning chunk of dry dung. When he saw Father, Kalu became guarded. Right behind him came Ramsahay, Ganeshi on his hip. At his heels, in his footsteps.

Father sat down cross-legged. The burning chunk of dung flared like molten iron in a blacksmith's furnace. Father sprinkled water from a small pot in a circle around the dung. He said, 'Kalu, bring that chunk of liver.' Kalu got up, took the piece of liver from a pile of chopped meat lying in a bowl nearby, and handed it to him. Father glanced at the knife and, on cue, Ramsahay quickly bent, picked it up, and gave it to him. Father cut the liver into two or three pieces and placed them on the burning dung. In a moment, the scent of roasted meat spread with a sizzling sound across the entire terrace. The breeze hastened the roasting, and the aroma filled our nostrils. Suddenly, the memory of a relative's cremation a month earlier floated into my mind. Almost everyone had moved out of the direction of the wind to escape the stench of the burning body. Some had covered their mouths with a handkerchief. Now my mouth filled with saliva – I got up and spat off one side of the terrace. Meanwhile, Father picked up a liquor bottle he'd bought and sprinkled a few drops around the flame and some into it.

'Ramesar, you won't of course kneel and pray. Your Babasaheb has forbidden you,' Father said, looking at me. And yet, he waited, watching me for several moments. I didn't stir from my chair. He was the only one who still called me Ramesar. Everyone, including Ma, called me by my new name, Avinash. I didn't have any quarrel with the manner of Father's puja. At least, there wasn't any need for a priest to broker between him and his god. It was a simple thing, but Father held on to old customs like a skilled butcher bearing down on the neck of an animal as it tried to wriggle free. Seeing that I had no reaction, he said to Ramsahay, 'Come, kneel and pay your respects.' As soon as he heard this, Ramsahay set Ganeshi down and bowed reverently.

Father got up to call out to Ma, 'Arrey, can you hear me, Ramsahay's ma? Bring Kusan over here and make him pay his respects.'

'He's sleeping. Don't bother him. He's got a fever,' I interjected firmly, and Father glared at me. He stayed quiet. So did I, without stirring from my chair.

'There must be at least four or five kilos?' Father asked Kalu.

'Yes, maybe a little more,' he said, lifting the pan and gauging its contents. He still didn't get up – he had reached for the pan from his squatting position, waddling like a duck.

'I find the bazaar meat bland, Brother Kalu.' This was Father.

'Bhai Saheb, they mostly butcher sheep. And sheep never taste as good. But everyone cheats,' Kalu said.

Dusk had started to descend. The sky, continually shifting colours, began to turn black. The moon had risen early, looking tired and defeated. Kalu was still sitting on his haunches. He had gotten up once to pee, but resumed his position as if he had never left it at all. It seemed as though he had been sitting there motionless forever. What a strange man. The sight of him sitting in such an awkward posture began to irritate me. Father picked up the liquor bottle and walked up the stairs toward the barsati, the room on the roof. I had so much to ask Kalu, but before I could utter a word, Father's voice called, 'Kalu! Come up here. Ramsahay's brought the roast liver.'

Kalu promptly started climbing the stairs when he heard Father's voice. I was left alone. I took a good look at Kalu as he climbed. There was barely any flesh on his body. He had no fat either, and his skin sagged on his bones like a flimsy, loose curtain. I was lost in a reverie. Anita's arrival disrupted my train of thought.

'Avinash, take this upstairs to Papa,' she said.

'Did you make it?' I asked.

'Not me, Papa's darling daughter-in-law did. You think he'd eat anything I made?' Anita said, laughing. It wasn't a natural laugh. It was filled with sarcasm and pain.

The stars were dim. A thin mist had spread everywhere. It had grown colder. I got up and, taking the plate of fried liver, began distractedly to climb the stairs barefoot. Father's and Kalu's voices were filtering through the windows.

'So Archana died. How?' I heard Father say. He sighed with surprise, grief, and the pain of an old wound. As soon as I heard the name, I halted. I couldn't proceed.

'Brother, the poor girl died in spirit a long time ago. Her body gave in only now. It's been a year.' This was Kalu's voice, full of irony and pity. Coloured by liquor.

'She was ill-fated, poor thing. You, of course, had come to Delhi. Her wedding was just a couple of weeks after yours. Who'd call it a marriage…it was utter injustice. The headmaster was such a good man. You know well, Bhai Saheb, what a gentleman he was. Such goodness turned his own community against him. His relatives had arranged the match for Archana. The headmaster saw to everything, leaving nothing undone. I too went to the feast. He had invited people from all castes. I met Archana as well. She asked about you. She also asked what your wife was like and if she was beautiful. When I said yes, she asked, 'More than me?' How could I lie? I said no.' Out on the stairs, I could hear his hesitant voice.

'Her wrists were bandaged. When I asked what had happened, she said she'd got cut. Then she started crying. Seeing her cry, I started to weep too. She held me in her lap. 'When your brother comes, tell him Archana died,' she said through her tears. She got married, but what can one do when happiness is not in your fate?' Kalu went quiet after this. Perhaps he was taking a swig.

'You have no idea, Kalu, what a sham my own marriage was. What happened then?' The memory of an old love throbbed in Father's voice.

'She had just left for her husband's home, and two days later, she was a widow. Her husband jumped in front of a train. People said he was impotent...no idea if that was true or not.' Then, whispering, he said, 'Some people even dragged your name into this. They said that Ramjilal had had his fun and tossed the leftovers to another, and that's why he died. Damned idiots – they babble whatever comes to their mind.' Then Kalu was quiet again. No voice came from the room for a few moments.

'What about Archana?' Father's words tumbled indistinctly from the window.

'What about her...people said that her damned in-laws were absolute monsters. They shaved her head. They starved her. These upper caste people are really cruel. Among us, if a woman becomes a widow, she can remarry. No one would think of shaving her head. People also said that her father-in-law was hell-bent on destroying her honour. Wretched widower. When the headmaster went to bring her back, her father-in-law insulted him. The headmaster was a good man. Such good souls have it tough. He returned quietly, without a fuss. His relatives didn't help him.' I heard Kalu take a deep drag on his bidi.

'Her hair was just like silk. It reached down to her waist. You saw it, Kalu,' Father's voice was distraught.

'Forget about me, Bhai Saheb, what did I not see? I saw you and her doing a lot of things...' As he said this, he took a heavy drag. He must have winked with his left eye again. I had found it repugnant. Father must not have liked it either. But perhaps his attention wasn't on Kalu's eye at this moment. It was on the pain of love.

'So she just stayed there?' Father's voice sounded as though it came from the bottom of a very deep well.

'What else? The bastards never let her go home. Her father-in-law had his fangs into her. Why would he have spared her? But seven or eight months later, she was found one evening lying outside the village in the balai neighbourhood. Her whole body was black and blue. She had been badly beaten. Her fucking in-laws had beaten her up and abandoned her when no one was looking. The balais recognised her as soon as they saw her. They called the headmaster. Then they took her home. She got better in a few weeks, but her father couldn't bear to see her sadness. Three or four months later, he suddenly died. So terrible was his grief that he died, resting in his chair, wasted away from within. The good man died a peaceful death.' Kalu was shaken by a violent cough and kept coughing for a long time. He coughed until he lost his breath. Then, suddenly, it stopped. I suppose Father must have given him some water. Even though I wanted to, I couldn't go inside. I was still holding the plate of roast liver.

'Archana had a mother – what about her? Had she already passed away?' Father's voice was drenched in grief. I had never heard him speak in such a tone. This wasn't the voice of the butcher-father I knew so well; it was full of love and actually seemed human. This aspect of Father, his voice aching with love, was completely unrecognisable to me.

'No, the headmaster's wife was still alive. She died a few years after he did. In the beginning, they suffered a lot. The household ran on the headmaster's pension. Archana became a nurse. She later tried hard to get a job as a teacher, but she didn't succeed. Perhaps her biggest misfortune befell her even later. How can meat in a kite's nest be safe?...

My tongue freezes, I can't tell you.' Kalu stopped speaking. My ears pricked up, even more intent.

'What happened?' Father asked.

'The worst that could happen to a woman,' he said and was quiet again. No voice came now from within. Then Father asked again, and Kalu said in a heavy voice, 'The bastards destroyed her honour. One night, she was on her way back from work at a neighbouring village's dispensary. They pounced on the opportunity. People said that it was boys from her own family who raped her. This is how the upper castes live, isn't it, Bhai Saheb? You know, there is a Mahatmaji who visits the village. Kundalnathji. He used to say that such things have always been common among these folk. Their holy books are full of stories about brothers doing sisters, and fathers raping daughters. He also explained many other things. Mahatmaji said that our ancestors created words like sisterfucker and daughterfucker for the ancestors of the upper castes – for that's what they did. Then they turned them into insults. We had heard about it among the Muslims. About girls being married off to their cousins. But this was no damn wedding. The scum had foul intentions from the very start. Mahatmaji said their scriptures called this a monstrous *rakshasa* wedding. Rakshasa wedding means by force, Bhai Saheb.' Maybe he was waiting for Father to press further before he said more. I knew Father wouldn't be able to.

Again a voice slipped out of the room. It was Kalu's. 'The

headmaster's wife died a few days later, of shock. The police and the court got involved. Eight low caste boys were accused – five balais, two of our khatiks, and also one bhangi. Two were sentenced to eight years. The rest went in for two. They'd got Archana to sign some papers. The poor girl was out of her senses. I used to visit her. No one stopped me. Later, she asked about you and your wife a couple of times, but you weren't even visiting the village.

'Six months later, she moved into the balai neighbourhood. Bhai Saheb, tell me, if the balais had raped her, would she have gone to live there? She wouldn't, right? The balais gave her a lot of support, actually. She lived there until she breathed her last. She had a daughter. That was a year later...' He was quiet again.

'Everyone keeps telling us that balais are thieves...' Father's voice was subdued, heavy with deep regret. 'Where is her daughter now?' His voice sounded broken.

'She's still there. Archana got her married to Chaina Balai's boy. The boy was an officer in the police department. Archana's daughter became a college lecturer. The brahmins and baniyas mocked them. They called Archana mad. But she wasn't crazy, she was very wise. She had come to hate her own people.' Kalu laughed. This set off another coughing fit. He kept on coughing. Perhaps Father gave him water once again. But this time the coughing wouldn't stop. Then suddenly it did. Father called out, 'Ramsahay!'

I raced into the room, and my eyes nearly popped out. Uncle Kalu lay on the floor. His eyes were rolled back in his head. I looked for his pulse, it was still there. I bent down and listened to his heart, it was still beating. He was unconscious. I ran downstairs and called for Ramsahay. We quickly lifted him into the car and rushed to the hospital. Father came with us. We brought him to the emergency room. Ramsahay, Father, and I nervously paced outside. It must have been around 8 p.m. Half an hour later, the senior doctor stepped out.

'The chances of saving him are very slim. He's sinking. We will try our best, but…both his lungs are damaged. Completely. And on top of that, he has had too much to drink. Did he want to die? This isn't an accident, it's suicide. Alcohol is absolute poison for him. He's regained a little consciousness now. Who is Bhai Saheb?' The doctor said to me and motioned us to come inside. Father followed him, and I went along with him. Seeing us come in, Uncle Kalu folded his hands as he lay there.

'Forgive me, Bhai Saheb. I am troubling you even as I die.'

Father enveloped Kalu's hands in his own.

'Don't be silly, brother. You'll be fine. I'll handle your treatment. I won't let anything happen to you at least. I'll stake all my wealth. Don't worry.' As he spoke, Father's eyes welled up with tears. Kalu's eyes were moist as well.

'I don't have anyone left. Maybe I was fated to die here. Don't take my ashes to the Ganga after I'm cremated. I've taken initiation from Mahatmaji,' he said, faltering. His voice was getting increasingly feeble.

'I knew that alcohol was poison for me. But what could I do? It wasn't a worse poison than solitude. You have wonderful children, Bhai Saheb. Let them live their lives. Even animals let their children be once they grow up. Having children is a great happiness in itself, Bhai Saheb.' As he spoke, tears streamed down his cheek.

'Stop talking now. You'll be fine. Don't lose heart. I'll take you to the best hospital. I won't let you go so easily.' Despite his encouraging words, Father couldn't stop himself from crying. His eyes welled up time and again. Uncle Kalu smiled.

'I miss Piloo a lot. It seems like he is still waiting for me. He was my child. My tender, beautiful kid. Kaka didn't spare him either. I held his feet down, brother. My own child's. I'm such a butcher!' He started crying, hiccupping.

'Is Khusnan outside?' he asked softly when he stopped crying.

'Enough! Now please leave, all of you.' A Malayali nurse ordered us out in a strange, accented Hindi when she saw him crying. Perhaps she knew he wouldn't make it, and that's why she'd given us so much time with him.

Father and I stepped out. It was 10 p.m. Father sent Ramsahay home. The store had to be opened in the morning. At almost 11 p.m., the doctor came out and told us flatly of Kalu's suicide. 'He is no more. Collect the body from the mortuary in the morning. This was a hopeless case.' The doctor walked away to his cabin down the corridor, chuckling and chatting with a junior doctor.

'Let's go home, Father, there's nothing we can do until morning,' I said.

'You go. I'll stay here,' he said.

'What about food?' He didn't respond, and there was no point asking again. I went home. I lay awake the whole night. I told Anita to go to sleep. She and Kushan slept soundly, without a care. One incident touches different people in many different ways. All night, Kalu's words sputtered in my head like whirling firecrackers. The process that turns an innocent child into a cruel adult; the social calamities that befell Archana; Father's dreams and the reality that transformed him from a person of love into a brutal butcher...I kept mulling over these things all night. Elsewhere, Father – alone, hungry – spent the whole night at the hospital. The night slid past.

It was a long night. Father returned home in the morning.

'Avinash,' came Father's faint voice at the door. Broken. The name sounded strange coming from him. I went to him. He was slouched listlessly on the sofa.

'Is Anita awake yet?' he asked, without meeting my eyes. To hear Anita's name from Father's lips felt like an explosion. A marvellous surprise. Father's tone today resembled the way he spoke last night. In the last eight years, he'd never once asked after Anita.

'Yes, she's awake. Tell me.' I said.

'I'll have some tea.' Father lay down on the sofa. I stared at him, speechless. His brow was relaxed, unfurrowed.

Yes Sir

'Tiwari! Some water!'

To Ramnarayan Tiwari, outside at his post on a corridor stool, the very sound of Deputy General Manager Narottam Saroj's deep voice was like having mercury poured down his throat. Never in his twenty-two years of service had he been in such a situation. Whenever Narottam called for him, Tiwari felt an intense pressure in his bowels. He jerked his head to one side to dissipate the unease. The feeling had plagued him all the past year – its onset dating, in fact, to Narottam Saroj's promotion from Assistant General Manager to Deputy General Manager a year ago.

'Scum! He doesn't even have regard for age. He must be at least a dozen years my junior. He was made an officer under the quota – the pawn becomes a knight, and there's pride in his stride! If it weren't for the quota, he'd be pushing a broom somewhere,' Tiwari muttered to himself as he scurried into the room. All these thoughts flew into his head the instant he heard the sound 'Ti'; by the time he heard 'wari', he had already opened the door. He could feel himself getting warm, despite the pleasant cool of the Delhi October.

'Yes sir,' is what he said, but the words scraped against his tongue. He felt as though he were being plunged into a deep well. He consoled himself with visions of Narottam being transferred, a possibility he never failed to petition for during the morning prayers he performed daily in strict adherence to family custom. Sometimes it crossed his mind to ask Vishnu for the demon's death, but, as he stoically told himself, such recourse was not in his upbringing. After all, Tiwari reasoned, what harm has he really done me?

To further effect the transfer, Tiwari had on several occasions organised recitations of the Satyanarayan katha, the ritual retelling of the travails a devotee endured to win the favor of Lord Satyanarayan. Every day Tiwari went to work hoping he would reach office and find Narottam gone. But this dream was never realised.

'Are you just going to stand there? Here, fill this with water,' Narottam kept working without raising his eyes. He was writing something. There was no especial harshness in this order, but Tiwari felt hurt nonetheless. He had many a time thought of poisoning Narottam's water. But this remained only a thought.

'The wretch fancies himself descended from the British. He even brings his coffee and his water in a thermos from home in his car. Says he doesn't trust the water here,' Tiwari thought, shifting from foot to foot.

'Have you ever seen an RO, Tiwari? We've had one at our place for years,' Narottam said, outraging Tiwari with his arrogance. 'So, tell me, Tiwari, what does RO mean?' Narottam stopped writing in his file and fixed Tiwari with a cool stare.

Under his gaze, Tiwari felt like a worm. 'RO is a type of Aquaguard, sir,' he answered cautiously. He didn't want to look like an idiot.

Narottam exploded. 'You know, this is exactly what's wrong with you people – donkeys, horses, everything's the same! If you want to buy toothpaste, you'll say, 'I'm going to buy Colgate,' and if you want detergent, you'll say, 'I'm buying Surf.' Arrey, you dimwit, Aquaguard is the name of a company. It's called a water purifier. A machine that cleans water and an RO system are two different things. Haven't you seen it on TV? They have an ad with *Dreamgirl* Hema Malini and her two daughters to sell it.' As he said this, Narottam uncharacteristically smiled a little. He almost never smiled.

Tiwari smiled too, but the word 'dimwit' had pierced him like a spear.

Tiwari had spent the first eighteen years of his life in his ancestral village. People from ten surrounding villages engaged his father, Pandit Shivnarayan Tiwari, for priestly services. He hadn't severed his connection with the village even now. In fact, his eldest son was born there – Tiwari had brought his wife from the city for the delivery. Whenever he visited, he forgot he was just a peon in a public sector office of the Indian government. As soon as he stepped off the bus he was shown the reverence that was his due. The village was about a kilometre from the bus stand, but walking this distance was a pleasure, even in the scorching sun. Every ten steps, someone or the other greeted him reverentially or touched his feet.

To this day, Tiwari hadn't told anyone in the village that he worked as a peon in Delhi. He had three justifications to soothe his conscience.

First, how was it anyone's business what work he did in the city? Second, what right did he have to taint the name of his father, Pandit Shivnarayan Tiwari, famed across ten villages for his recitations of the Satyanarayan katha and Tulsidas' *Ramcharit Manas*? And third, he did not have the right to destroy the innocent faith of the villagers by telling them that their revered brahmin god washed the dirty dishes of his officers in the city. They would incur sin were they merely to hear of such a thing. Therefore, he referred to himself as a clerk, a babu, and some people in the village had started calling him babuji. The greeting, 'Babuji, I touch your feet,' gratified him more than 'Panditji, I touch your feet.' Ever since he'd patted Bhima Valmiki on the shoulder and asked how he was doing, his stature had grown manifold in the village. 'Who's humble and who's noble? We're all human,' he would say magnanimously, invoking Guru Nanak. 'The whole world emerged from a single light.'

'RO means Reverse Osmosis,' Narottam said, and Tiwari's mouth fell open. His eyes narrowed, and his brow knotted. Tiwari felt like a student at the feet of his guru.

'Okay, forget it. Pour me some coffee and leave now,' Narottam dismissed him.

'Yes sir.' There was deference in Tiwari's voice. He felt relieved. 'Some day when he orders coffee from outside, I'll poison it, or at least I'll spit into it...I swear by my departed father that I'll serve it to him polluted.' But whenever the odd opportunity presented itself, he had not been able to bring himself to do it. Instead, he took great care when serving coffee, covering the cup with a saucer. He didn't take such care with his own tea. Time and again he cursed his own words and deeds. Sometimes because he couldn't bring himself to act upon his thoughts, and sometimes because he hated himself for wishing such things upon another human being. It wasn't humane. But was it humane to curtly order around a man ten to twelve years your elder?

'He must be just seven or eight years older than my son.' For a moment, the face of his handsome son came to his mind. Tall and fair-skinned with broad shoulders, curly black hair, brown eyes, a high forehead, and a pointed nose...a twenty-year-old who had graduated with first class honours. 'And this lowlife here has risen to this level only because of the quota system,' he spat to himself.

'Now, how long will you hang around here, Tiwari?' Narottam's voice remained stern, but there was a faint smile around his lips. Tiwari felt himself burn.

'Go and give this file to Mishraji...and come back quick.' Narottam tossed the file on the table. 'Don't linger anywhere.'

'Yes sir, I mean, no sir.' He was confused. 'Tell me, sir, when do I ever dilly-dally?' Tiwari spoke in an exaggeratedly sycophantic voice. He was surprised at his own tone. Who was this speaking from inside him? Why was he kowtowing to this lowborn scum? As he left the room, he became aware of his stooping shoulders. He pulled in his stomach, straightened his spine, and pushed out his chest as far as he could.

He entered Assistant General Manager Rammurti Mishra's room.

'Sir...'

'Hmm?' Mishra was immersed in his work; he hadn't noticed Tiwari enter. When he heard Tiwari's voice, he raised not just his eyes but his whole head. People who wear glasses often have to lift their whole head to be able to see.

'File.' Tiwari put the file on the table. His voice was aggrieved and he wanted Mishra to notice this, so he also made his face despondent.

'Anything else?' Mishra asked brusquely and started to write something.

'What else, saheb, *kaliyug* is here. Brahmins are forced to wash the dirty dishes of the lowborn,' Tiwari tried to rouse Mishra.

'So, quit then! Are you working here on doctor's orders? Go back to the village and beg for a living.'

Mishra's harsh voice frightened him. 'No sir, that wasn't what I meant. I mean, shouldn't we find it disturbing that a low-caste quota case gives us orders when a learned brahmin like you should have been in his seat?'

Tiwari had played his hand well – a troubled look came over Mishra's face. Then he checked himself and simply said, 'Hmm,' but he put his pen down. He was distracted. He had lost his focus.

'The lowborn spoke so insolently to you the other evening – he just threw those files at you…' Tiwari latched on to Mishra's sinking mood.

'This was bound to happen,' Mishra's voice sounded more resigned than frustrated. He felt the ache of an old wound. 'Yesterday's servant boy today sits on our heads. He's got an MBA, and now he thinks he can piss all over us? I've been toiling away for twenty years to get here. He's only a year or two older than my daughter. If it weren't for the quota, where would he be?' Mishra sighed deeply.

'He is very arrogant, sir. He never talks to anyone, just keeps sitting there silently all day. And when he does speak, it's always from a high horse.' Tiwari's voice was smouldering. 'Did you know he passed in the third division?' Tiwari lowered his voice as if he were telling a secret.

'Yes, I know.' Now Mishra's voice was glum. He was thinking of the day when Narottam told him of his struggles to get his MBA. Despite the sting of a third division BA, he had studied night and day and had passed his MBA at his first attempt. 'The day begins when you wake up', was Narottam's motto.

'Arrey, saheb, the bastard's a real low-life,' Tiwari's courage grew as he vented his anger.

'Alright, get out now.' Mishra's voice was suddenly sharp. His harshness put Tiwari in his place. Tiwari understood his mistake and turned to go.

'Oh, and listen, I've told you several times to knock and ask to be let in before entering,' Tiwari looked back and saw Mishra was once again absorbed in his work, just like Narottam.

'Bastard…this is why he was outcasted in his village.' Tiwari started spitting insults at Mishra as he left the room. The wall-clock caught his eye. 'Arrey! It's already twelve!'

'Panditji, namaskar!' Tiwari turned and saw Durgadas Valmiki sprawled on a sofa near the storeroom. He was waving Tiwari over. Tiwari walked toward him dejectedly. Durgadas did not rise as he approached, angering Tiwari all the more.

'What's up, panditji? You wander about all day, you must be tired. Why don't you sit for a while?' Although Durgadas was in his mid-fifties, three floors of janitorial labour kept him fit.

'Want a cigarette?'

Tiwari sat next to him. Durgadas pushed a golden packet of 555 toward him, and Tiwari's eyes shone.

'Where'd you pinch these from, eh?' The words fell spontaneously from Tiwari's mouth. He briskly put his hand out, took a cigarette, and smoothly placed it between his lips.

'You too, panditji? What pinching? Saheb gave them to me.'

'Which saheb?' Tiwari lit the cigarette, stretched his legs out, and started to puff the way Chief General Manager Abhaysingh Dabas did. He got a slight head rush.

'Arrey, panditji, the one who bought twenty pigs of mine yesterday, that saheb.' Durgadas cupped his cigarette in his fist and took a deep drag.

When he heard Durgadas' words, the cigarette nearly fell from Tiwari's lips. An acrid taste suffused his mouth. He wanted to throw the cigarette away and give Durgadas a piece of his mind.

'Was he Punjabi?' Tiwari asked hopefully.

'Arrey, panditji, you're all-seeing. That's why I respect you so much.' Durgadas patted Tiwari's knee.

Hearing this, Tiwari found his breath again. He took two quick puffs and fought off his nausea. He stretched out his legs once more, turned his face toward the ceiling, and started to draw on his cigarette, just like CGM Dabas.

'Yeah, he was someone called Chopra Saheb, the business partner of a distant in-law of mine. If you saw my in-law, you'd say he was Kashmiri. Fifteen years ago, Chopra Saheb started a pig farm with a government loan, and now the bastard's rolling in dough.' Durgadas' face betrayed regret, pride, and rivalry.

'He was trying to provoke me, waving his 555s at me like I'd never seen one before. But, guruji, I caught on. I'm a first-rate sneak, so I grabbed the whole packet and asked to keep it. The bastard was in a bind. He said arrogantly, 'Keep it, keep it.' But I knew very well that the packet was Chopra Saheb's.'

'Durga, you've got a decent job. What's the need for you to get into this pig-farming business? Kick such nasty work aside.' Tiwari had recovered.

'Arrey, panditji, don't say such inauspicious things. Pigs are our children, our fortune. It's because of them that we make a little profit. Don't people raise cows, buffalos, sheep, and goats? Raising our pigs is just the same. Work is work, how can it be dirty or lowly? Money doesn't smell. Chopra does the same work. It's just a difference in scale, panditji. When you do sweepers' work on a large scale, there's no shame in that either.' Tiwari's words had touched a nerve.

'As you please. I have to go now. It's time for saheb's coffee.' Tiwari sensed Durgadas' discomfort. He ground his cigarette out on the floor and flicked the butt under the couch.

'Could I take another?' Tiwari pressed down hard on his knees for support and stood up.

'Here, take two, panditji.' Durgadas held out the packet. Tiwari extracted two cigarettes and returned the pack.

Tiwari hurried back to Narottam's room and stood outside the door. He looked at the clock. 12:10. He was ten minutes late with the coffee. The scum would surely yell at him. As he thought about this, he rolled down his cuffs and buttoned them at his wrists.

'That ass sits there running the air conditioner even in this cold weather,' Tiwari clucked like a chicken. 'May I come in, saheb?' His voice was unctuously polite.

'Yes, and take a look at the air conditioner. What's it on?' Narottam was busy on the computer.

'Saheb, it's on twenty-two.'

'Put it up to twenty-eight. Do you need to wait for instructions even for a routine job? The weather is changing, but you menial workers have thick skin, I suppose. How would you know?' His eyes were still fixed on the computer.

'Bastard, asshole, dog, lowborn, scum...The father's not killed so much as a frog, and the son's a marksman!' Tiwari's mind rang with every insult he could remember. He thought of the previous Deputy General Manager, Manohar Patel. Manohar Patel had never called Tiwari by name. Let alone making him do the dishes, Patel did not even ask him to fetch water. He just had him deliver files here and there. Those days, Tiwari had it good. The officers used to come in first, and the peons arrived later – but no one complained. The trouble started when the office installed a punch-in machine. Ever since then, everyone had to be in by nine o'clock.

Tiwari had cursed this new machine for a long time. Even today, whenever someone mentioned it, it was like scratching at an old wound. 'Here, Tiwari.' Tiwari raised his eyes toward Narottam, who held out two sheets of paper. His hand reached toward Tiwari, but his eyes were still glued to his screen.

Tiwari took the papers quietly, apprehensively. The writing on them was in English. Nevertheless, when the content is of import, even Chinese can be deciphered. He wanted to shout out, but he couldn't. He squealed happily instead: 'You are so kind, sir! May you live long, sir! May you prosper, may your status grow manifold!' On one sheet, Narottam had praised Tiwari's assiduousness and good character at length, and had recommended him for promotion to the position of clerk. This letter was addressed to CGM Abhaysingh Dabas. The second letter was from the CGM, in which he gave his assent for the promotion.

'Are you happy?' Narottam pushed his revolving chair toward Tiwari.

In spite of the condescending 'tu' Narottam used to address him, Tiwari's eyes shone with gratitude. They took in Narottam's figure for the first time: his dark, shining complexion, small nose, thick black hair, and large, soot-coloured eyes. Fat eyebrows, a bushy moustache, a slender neck, strong shoulders, and a light blue suit…Narottam's person seemed magnificent to him.

'You look just like Lord Ram, sir.' Words of gratitude tumbled from Tiwari's mouth. 'How much of a raise will I get?'

'About two thousand.' Narottam's voice was full of tenderness and enthusiasm, like hot, puffed rotis.

When he heard this, sweet music played in Tiwari's ears. He carefully poured coffee from the thermos into a cup. When he saw Narottam engrossed again at the computer, he tiptoed out gingerly so his shoes wouldn't squeak. Once outside, he shut the door with care, not letting it make a single sound.

He showed his paper in almost every cabin. He still couldn't calm down. First he thought he'd surprise his wife in the evening; he would be calmer on seeing her eyebrows arch in surprise. After wandering restlessly for a while, he decided that there was no harm in telling her now. But he didn't just telephone his wife; he also called his brother, brother-in-law, sister-in-law, and his aunt and uncle. He called each one in turn, enquired after their health, and, towards the end, casually shared the news of his becoming a clerk. They all congratulated him heartily, but his peace of mind had completely disappeared. Lost in himself, he somehow managed to serve the saheb lunch and eat his own as well.

'Okay, there's just one hour left,' Tiwari looked at the clock and muttered. The clock said 4:30.

'Tiwari!' Narottam's voice invaded his solitude. He got up as though mesmerised and entered the room reverently. Now this voice neither pierced him nor made him tremble with anger.

'My friend, go and call the sweeper. What's his name?'

'Sir, Layakram.'

'Yes, that fellow. Look at this mess,' Narottam's eyes narrowed.

Tiwari walked toward the toilet. The toilet was blocked, and water was flowing onto the floor and into the room.

'Where is this water coming from?' Wondering, Tiwari turned his attention to a tap that was slowly dripping. He leaned forward to turn the tap, and the water started flowing faster.

'Sir, the tap's washer has come loose,' Tiwari shouted from the toilet.

'Yeah, I know.' Narottam evinced agreement without stirring from his seat.

Tiwari managed somehow to tighten the tap. The water was dripping slowly once again. Squelching, he emerged from the toilet, wiped his shoes on the mat, and left the room. He went searching for Layakram from one room to the next, and then from one floor to the other, looking in all the places he might be, but he couldn't find him.

'Driver's room!' The idea suddenly flashed in his mind. He arrived at the driver's room on the ground floor, where Layakram could often be found killing time. Where his buddy, Sardar Lucky Singh, also hung out.

'Oye, pandit, come over here!' Lucky Singh shouted as soon as he spotted Tiwari.

'Where's your buddy, eh sardar?' Tiwari knew that these two ate together and drank together. He sounded irritated.

'Oh, I've been looking for that bastard too...who knows where he's run off to today.' Lucky Singh was seething. It was evening, and his drinking buddy was missing.

Tiwari understood that Layakram was nowhere in the office. Even had he been, he would have been drunk at this hour. As if observing some religious rule, he started drinking at four every day. In this matter he was punctilious. All the officers knew about it, but no one did a thing. Once he told the fax operator, Sheila Taneja, that she had a nice backside. Sheila filed a written complaint, but for some reason, General Manager R.S. Jain saved him. Layakram had fallen at Sheila's feet and asked for forgiveness. Two days later, he had walked into Sheila's fax room and urinated. He was drunker than ever. No one dared cross him after that.

So Tiwari started searching everywhere for Durgadas Valmiki. Though he knew that cleaning toilets wasn't Durgadas' job, Tiwari figured he wouldn't have a problem with it – he was a valmiki after all. But even after searching through all three floors, he couldn't find Durgadas. Defeated, he sat down opposite the typist, Rina Sawhney.

'What's wrong, Tiwari?' Rina fixed her lipstick and snapped her compact mirror shut. She was primping before leaving the office, just as she did in the mornings before leaving home.

'This is just how these Scheduled Caste people are, Tiwari,' Rina struck a blow after she heard him out.

'No, no, madam, they're not all alike,' Tiwari was quick in his defense, and he stood up.

'Why don't you call Durga on his mobile?' Rina suggested, and

Tiwari slapped his forehead. 'Uff...that hadn't even occurred to me!'

'Arrey, Durgadas bhai, where are you?' Tiwari took pains to sound gentle.

'Panditji, I've just arrived at Sarojini Nagar. Jain Saheb sent me.'

'When will you be back?' Tiwari sounded more impatient now.

'Can't say,' said Durgadas, and the line was cut.

This was a flat-out lie. Durgadas was sitting in the basement car park, playing cards. Lucky Singh, having given up waiting for Layakram, had headed down there in search of another drinking companion. He told everyone about Tiwari's predicament. After that, Durgadas didn't stick around. He kick-started his motorcycle and left. He didn't even stop for a quick peg.

'Saheb, neither Layakram nor Durgadas is anywhere to be found,' Tiwari reported to Narottam, despite his fear that Narottam might make him take care of the problem.

'Okay, you can go. Tell Layakram about it tomorrow,' Narottam was busy reading a file.

'Why don't I do it, sir...you'll be unnecessarily bothered,' the words tumbled from Tiwari's mouth. Tiwari was surprised and troubled... who was this damned lowborn speaking from inside him?

'You?' Narottam's eyes met Tiwari's for the first time. 'Why should you be needlessly troubled?' There was a mixture of respect, astonishment, and confusion in this unexpected question.

'Why not, sir?…Doesn't the bathroom get blocked at our home…? I'll just poke at it with a stick, and it'll be settled.' As he said this, Tiwari stepped into the toilet.

A sound emerged from the toilet – *gharr-ghurr-gharr-ghurr*. 'What shame is there in work, sir?' Tiwari called out between the gurgles.

After waiting a few minutes, Narottam asked, 'Is the water going down, Tiwari?'

Tiwari's joyful voice emerged like the buzzing of a fly. 'It's going down all right, sir, slowly.'

New Custom

The man's nostrils quivered, blasted by stench. As soon as he alighted from the bus, his nose collided with the smell, while his eyes met the form of a man lying naked in the distance. Was there a relationship between the two? He thought about it for a moment, but it was hard to make a connection because the odour – whether of rotting flesh or soured milk – was coming from the opposite direction.

The bus stand was quite deserted. The wind was exceedingly cold; the man shivered despite his warm coat. Of their own, his hands sought out the warmth of his trouser pockets, only to quickly re-emerge to tighten his rust-coloured muffler. Romila had insisted on wrapping it around his neck as he left, the same way she sometimes put her arms lovingly around him. His conscience stirred, and he wondered why he was always in a fault-finding mood with her. It depressed him.

He wanted to wrap the muffler around his ears – it would surely have brought him some relief – but he couldn't. People who wore mufflers around their ears were looked down on in the city; he would be jeered at with shouts of 'Hey Bihari! Oye Bihari!', which was yet another way of making people feel inferior. He preferred suffering the piercing wind to being branded a muffler-bundled Bihari.

It was well past nine in the morning, but because of the heavy fog, it seemed like night was gathering. The sun's rays could not penetrate the dense fog. There was just enough illumination to see as far as one's hands, but it was a drowsy light, not a lively one. A damp gleam was settling in all directions as though a big furry brown cat had stretched itself out.

There were only a few days left for spring, but this year the winter had shown no sign of relenting. All the newspapers and TV channels said the cold this season had broken a thirty-year record – the Meteorological Department's forecast had been proved wrong once again – and, interspersed with dispirited offerings of 'chewing-gum news', the channels were packed with ads for various national and international products to keep you from the cold. In one, a slender, beautiful girl hides her boyfriend from her father in a large fridge, where he is discovered happily eating ice cream. The cold doesn't bother him in the least because he wears the thermal undergarments the advertiser is promoting. A rival manufacturer shows how a young girl's devotion to a flabby old man causes his youthful nephew much heartache, upon which the man vainly and indecently leers that it is an 'inside' matter. A tonic advertisement features honeymooners raving about a saffron-containing product and the 'heat' it generates. This is a man's world, where women are treated like objects and men are deluded into believing themselves to be the consumers. In this game, it is hard to know who the product is and who the customer; everyone is stirred around in the same pot.

If he lowered his eyes a bit, they snagged on the naked man again. Was he dead? The question smouldered. He picked up his suitcase and walked in the man's direction. He stared straight ahead.

'Take a seat, darbar,' a voice broke his reverie.

A man at a roadside tea stall was watching him as he set an aluminum pot on a big stove. The stove was fired up and emitted a low, hissing sound, its flames making the blackened pot even blacker. The wayfarer shifted his attention from the pot with effort, his glance transfixed instead by a big chunk of fresh ginger lying on some greasy sacks near the man's fat, filthy feet.

Inwardly, he smiled when the shopkeeper called him 'darbar'. The man knew that this form of address was reserved for the Thakur landlords of the region. Perhaps the shopkeeper had assumed him to be one, going by his tall stature and broad frame. Or was it his thick moustache? Or perhaps it was a marketing strategy to flatter potential customers. But then why would a customer be gratified at being called 'darbar'?

'Tea,' said the traveller, surprising himself. Given how filthy the place was, how could he drink tea here? His own voice sounded alien to him. At home, he upbraided Romila for kneading dough without washing her hands after closing the bathroom door – a comparatively small matter. Romila's retort was that she had already washed her hands with soap in the bathroom washbasin, so why the fuss?

'You don't care for hygiene!' he would shout to cover his discomfiture. 'And you're obsessed with cleanliness!' she would squawk like a chicken in a coop.

The shopkeeper crushed some ginger and put it in the black water seething in the even blacker pot.

'I shouldn't watch this,' he thought and looked in the other direction. After all, he wanted to drink tea. Having taught for ten years at a famous university in the metropolis, he had acquired a special kind of pride and refinement. A short distance away from this stall was another, and then a third and a fourth, each with small black pots mounted on black stoves.

There were two puppies at the stall opposite that were keeping warm by wrestling each other. This entertained him, and he began to take an interest. The brown puppy, which was a little skinny but extremely feisty, sometimes pulled the white puppy's ear, or bit his tail, or stuck his teeth into his neck. The white pup was plump and dignified, and had a long mark like a saffron *tilak* on his forehead. He ran a little distance, whining *kuun-kuun ghoon-ghoon*, but then he got annoyed, flipped the skinny brown pup over, and stood on him. Some devout soul had tried to erase the difference between the two by putting a saffron tika on the brown puppy's forehead as well, but it was very light, and you could only see it if you looked hard enough. Across the way, their mother lay dozing.

'Here you are, darbar,' the shopkeeper's voice penetrated the man's intense concentration the way a spider enters its web, stalking its prey. When the shopkeeper repeated 'Darbar, tea' in a brisk voice, the man turned his attention toward him. The shopkeeper had a dusky, oily face that sported a vermilion tilak. His rotten teeth were stained black by paan masala. The man's attention moved to the streamers of poison-ous paan masala and tobacco packets hanging in the shop.

'This is how the English turned the Chinese into opium addicts.'

'What?' The shopkeeper could make no sense of the man's utterance.

'Nothing. So, how did you know...' he paused.

'What?'

'...that...I'm a darbar.' He turned his gaze from the shopkeeper's face and took a sip.

'Oh, that's easy, darbar. Seeing your coat and pants, and your commanding presence, anyone would know,' his voice was sycophantic.

'Are you one too?'

'No, not at all.' He was embarrassed. 'I'm a mali, darbar, a saini.' His hands were joined as though seeking forgiveness.

The traveller turned his head and started to drink his tea. His attention once again turned toward the roughhousing puppies and their mother, who had now lifted her head and was taking pleasure in her pups' wrestling.

He recalled the conversation he'd had with his father the night before he left home. 'No, even if you repeat it a hundred times, I still won't accept it…money changes everything…village, city, town…all of it.' He saw his father's emotional upheaval. 'You're wrong, thinking that we could ever live well without it.' He rubbed his finger and thumb together, signifying hard cash. 'Only with forbearance and piety – my foot! Is this so-called piety meant only for us?' He stamped angrily. 'All these righteous souls crave worldly possessions, which only come from hard work and are bought with money.'

'Still, be careful, everything is just as it was there…the change that money has wrought is the change you see on rocks in a riverbed.' A father is anyway weakened in the face of a grown-up son. The position of a young, salaried son is like a young lion's. His father inevitably starts to quietly accept the new order, like an old lion must.

'No, Papa, money changes everything.' His voice was firm.

'Hey, shoo! Get out of here!' The shopkeeper yelled, and the man snapped back to the present. The shopkeeper was chasing the puppies that had slipped under the tables set outside his stall.

'What's the population of this village?' he looked toward the shopkeeper.

'Which one? There are three villages, that's why this place is also called Tigaon, Tri-village. One is Vanla ki Dhani, then there is Rajgarh, and the third is Kiratgarh. Which one are you asking about?'

'Rajgarh.'

'There are about three thousand houses…there must be about twenty-five thousand people.'

'Twenty-five thousand…' he gaped. 'It's a pretty big village.'

'Yes, darbar, they say that three or four hundred years ago, it was the biggest trading centre of the area…now it's become a poor village.' The shopkeeper put his hands on his knees and stood up, then stepped down from the stall. He drew a long bamboo pole from under the stall, hung a fat electrical wire on it, and attached it to the government power cable above the stall.

'What is this?' the man laughed.

'Connection…' The shopkeeper simply shrugged his shoulders, came back inside and squatted down as before. He reached for a portable television set lying at the back of the stall, brought it forward, and switched it on. An ad came on with an aged film actress making a living selling a brand of chips.

'Do you have those?' the man asked the shopkeeper, cocking an eyebrow at the screen.

'Which, the chips or the heroine?' the shopkeeper snickered. The man disliked his lascivious joke and laughter.

The shopkeeper read the disapproval in his face. 'I have them!' He took down a basket hanging at the back of the stall, in which there were several kinds of chips – Kurkure, Bingo. 'Can't stock everything up front.' The shopkeeper hung the basket on a protruding nail at the entrance to his stall.

'There's mineral water too,' he gestured toward the bottled waters arranged there and muttered, 'Have you come to see the fort?' The shopkeeper was inclined to chat. In this cold, he didn't have any other customers. The man was the only traveller to get off the bus here.

The shopkeeper's question went unheard. On the television set, an international channel was now showing pictures of Saddam Hussein. American soldiers had arrested him in a bunker and were interrogating him, forcing him to open his mouth. The channel showed this scene over and over. America was making him an example to the world, issuing a warning of how they would similarly go after anyone who crossed them.

'You've come to see the fort, darbar?' The shopkeeper repeated his question.

'No, I've come for a wedding.' He took a sip of tea.

'At whose place?' The question got trapped in his eyebrows, the way a fly thrashes about when it is caught in someone's hair.

'Dharm Singhji's place.' The man straightened his back.

'Oh, I see, I had no idea there was a wedding at the darbar saheb's place.' He struck his forehead with his hand theatrically. 'Darbar saheb, my wife is right when she says I am so wrapped up in my work that I have no idea what's going on around me. Now, you tell me, what's a man to do? I leave the house in the morning and come back late at night. I slave away the whole day for two pieces of roti…and what do women do? They live off our earnings, they idly eat and sleep. On top of this, they complain, 'We have to do the cooking. If you'd have to cook you'd know.' I tell you…'

He stopped for a moment and started again. 'Believe me, when his elder daughter was married, I slogged real hard…I was young then.' He twirled his moustache. 'I even gave five cots and eight copper pots for the wedding party's stay…my whole family slept on the ground for five days…I mean, why not? After all, she's the daughter of the village. Her honour is ours…you have to think of every little detail.'

'Hmm.' The man was staring determinedly at the TV and trying to shut out the shopkeeper's chatter.

'You have to maintain the rules and customs of the village,' the shopkeeper jabbered on.

'Hmm,' said the man downing the last of his tea and putting the glass on the table.

'Dharm Singhji hasn't said a word about his daughter getting married,' the shopkeeper muttered quietly. 'How strange.'

'Not his daughter, his son.' The man took out a handkerchief and wiped his mouth.

'His son?' The question shot up through his eyebrows. 'Which Dharm Singhji are you talking about?'

'Dharm Singhji of Rajgarh,' the man's voice was soaked in indifference.

'But he doesn't have a son. God only gave the poor man two daughters,' the shopkeeper's voice was clammy with sorrow.

'Arrey, no, it's his son's wedding...the wedding party will go to Jivangarh tomorrow...today is the bhat, the rice ceremony.' This time the man's voice had a glimmer of apprehension. He was hoping he wasn't in the wrong place.

'You've got it wrong somehow.' There was harshness, conviction, and authority in the shopkeeper's voice. 'Not just Dharm Singhji, I know the entire village. There must be a mix-up.'

'Doesn't he work in the water-works department?' The man got irritated.

'Oh no! You're talking about Dharma Harijan, the operator,' the shopkeeper slapped his forehead. 'As if there could be a wedding in the village without my knowing!' The shopkeeper's voice was distant and rude.

'How much do I owe you?' Noting the shift in the shopkeeper's tone, the man pulled out a hundred-rupee note.

'Three rupees. But, brother, first wash the glass.' This in the shop-keeper's rudest tone yet.

'Why?' The man felt as though a bucket of water had been dumped on him. His own voice seemed to come from the bottom of a well.

'Why?! This is the custom of the village,' the shopkeeper shouted for any bystander to hear. 'A rise in status does not put an end to custom.'

The man stepped down from the stall. He suddenly thought of his father. He saw the naked man lying in the distance. He saw the puppies wrestling. A few people had gathered. It was as if he were naked among them. Their gaze scorched him.

'What's going on, Banwari?' a face from the crowd tossed out the question.

'See, Chaudhari, I had taken him to be a good man…it's not as if it's written on someone's forehead who is what. He could have told me at the outset that he has come to Dharma Harijan's place,' the shopkeeper answered rudely.

There was some hesitation among the bystanders when they saw the man's clothing and impressive stature. The shopkeeper's next question was meant to clinch the issue. 'Should I serve you tea now in a Harijan glass?'

'And if I hadn't told you…?' Under the weight of the insult, the words emerged with difficulty.

'If you hadn't said anything, the sin would have been on you. You don't drink from a cup once you've spotted a fly in it,' the shopkeeper shouted, raising his hands.

'Why are you being stubborn, brother? Just wash it, this is the custom here,' a man came forward.

'Why make an issue of it?' another asked.

'Do you wash it too?' He turned toward the voice and asked haughtily.

'Why should I?' The man was offended.

'So then why should I?' came the retort.

'He's going to get thrashed. The bastard's exposed.' The shopkeeper's war cry was not lost on the man.

'How much for this glass?' His jaw clenched in anger.

'Why?' The shopkeeper was surprised.

'Tell me how much it is.' His brows were drawn together.

'Ten…no, twenty rupees,' the shopkeeper inflated the price.

'Take this,' he thrust the hundred-rupee note at the shopkeeper. The father of the nation, Mahatma Gandhi, was smiling on the note, wrapped in a shawl. The shopkeeper quickly grabbed the money.

'Change.' His eyebrows were stretched taut.

The man took the change from the shopkeeper, put it in his pocket. Picking up the glass, he smashed it against the chabutra, the platform under the trees on which village folk sat for tea and chit-chat. *Chanaak* – shards of glass flew in all directions. Startled by the noise, the mother dog jumped away, and the naked man suddenly sat up.

The man bent down, picked up his suitcase, and started toward the village. A smile bloomed on the shopkeeper's face, a smile not unlike Gandhiji's on the note.

Subcontinent

S*avage wolves keep returning through the tunnel of history. 185 BCE, 3 September 1939, 30 January 1948…these are the marks of their poisonous teeth. The wolves' eyes sparkle in the dark – night is their crown, for fear grows in the night,' read my uncle from the book he was holding. We all listened wide-eyed, our hearts pounding.*

Quiet, continuing to himself…

What big eyes my grandmother had! Large, cool, brown, their whites a pale yellow in her dark, wrinkled face. She was so beautiful. My silent Amma. When she ran her calloused palm over my hair, I felt as though the past was crushing my happiness. I couldn't refuse her anything. I was the black star that lit Amma's brown eyes.

Papa brought my grandmother to the city after my grandfather's death. But Amma never really took to it. Not even with all Papa's cajoling. The thatch from the huts of her village was lodged in the dark wrinkles of her face. Thatch blackened by the soot and smoke of earthen stoves. And the growling of wolves and hyenas lingered in her mind. Amma never accepted Dadaji's death. Until her last breath, she believed it was the villagers' doing. One evening, in the fading light, wolves tore Dadaji to shreds as he returned home through the jungle. He had been a disgrace in the eyes of the village. Yet she could not accept the city from the time she first arrived until the day her breath finally left her. Only when she became dust like Dadaji could she be at home in every place on earth. With respect and dignity…in the village, in the city, everywhere. These wolves, these stories of wolves, these memories of Amma, all spin hurtling through my mind. Wedding…the village wedding. The village, the wolves…a pack of wolves…

Science tells us wolves and dogs share the same lineage. The Canidae family. But wolves prefer the jungle. They emerge in packs from the wild. And dogs…

My eyes opened, and I saw a broken piece of sky, quivering in the square of the window, trapped. An immense black cloud had seized the feeble sun and wrung it, breaking its legs. It seemed as if night were near, but suddenly a lone ray pierced the cloud like a horse and arced across the room. The whole room was a-shimmer in the din of its hooves as if lit by the wavering flame of an oil lamp, unsteady but intent on continuing to burn. Perhaps this horse did belong to the sun – the lone, seventh horse of the Sun God's Chariot. I looked at my watch. It was a quarter past five. I couldn't close my eyes. But I covered my face with a blanket.

'Aren't you getting up?' she said as she came and pulled the blanket away. 'Still sleeping or what?' As if by seeing my state, she had understood all. Maybe she thought I was just lying down with my eyes closed. Distracted, I paused for a moment and said, 'No…I don't know…yeah, I guess I dozed off.' Too much thinking wouldn't let me sleep. Squandered sleep, ravaged consciousness. Just a little light, the tiniest brightness. Ruins of light. Ashes of consciousness.

'Want some tea?' she asked.

'Umm…no…uh, okay, make it, make it.' I said the last words loudly to show that I was in control of myself. I wanted to reassure her that I was alright. She smiled. But her eyes did not sparkle the way they usually did – or maybe they were sparkling, but I couldn't see. She left. Her white T-shirt had a boy on the back, sticking a thumb in the air while he clutched a bottle of some foreign soft drink. I could see him until she turned into the kitchen. He was climbing my wife's back…in the fleece of some charming sheep? The thought disturbed me.

The darkness outside had started to fill the room. The red and black remains of the sun lay toward the west. I got up to turn on the light. The old neon light coughed like a tuberculosis patient seven or eight times before filling the room with a lacklustre glow, the yellow shade of mucus. How dark it had become outside. Because of the light within, the darkness without seemed even more impenetrable, even more foreboding. My glance fell on the English books on the bed's headboard: *Riddles in Hinduism* and *Art and Social Life*. Delhi…was this our home? Rajasthan was our ancestors' birthplace. Our motherland. But, really, what is ours there? I start to descend the crumbling steps of an old step-well, surrounded by withered vines. I keep going down.

Step by step. The mist is dense. *Sarrr...ssseeee...jjhannn*. One, two, three...twenty-five. Twenty-five steps down. *Guddup...guddup*.

'I lie at your feet, Maharaj. Forgive them. They won't do it again. They'll never do it again in my life. They erred, having lived in the city. Have mercy, my lords.' My grand-aunt, Dadaji's sister-in-law, whom I also called Amma, pressed her forehead against the feet of the six young men.

With a wolf's snarl, one among them said, 'Bloody old bitch, you think you can piss on our heads because you live in the city? This one has forgotten his caste. And she – she doesn't hold by such things, does she? Let this bitch have it too, Narayan.'

'Oh God, I'm done for! Maaaa! Forgive me, master, kind sir! It won't happen again!' As Amma wailed, one of them struck her head hard with a shoe, and she cried out again. Tears streamed down her cheeks. Now they were all laughing. Seeing them beat Amma with their shoes, Father tried to get up again. When they noticed him moving, they fell on him afresh. Sticks, fists, shoes – flailing without stop. I stood trembling. One of them slapped me across the face. Father was lying on the ground. Unconscious. Blood dripping, *thap-thap-thap*, from his forehead. A streak of blood spread all the way down his pyjama. My lip had been split open. It was still bleeding. I stood there quaking. I almost pissed my pants. It seemed like it would never end. Father lay at peace. His new white kurta was torn from his chest to his stomach.

Blood dribbled from his mouth. Father's dead, I thought. Seeing a body drenched in blood, that's the only thing an eight-year-old can think. I quietly wiped the blood off my lip with my torn collar. There were no tears in my eyes. But I kept making small crying sounds, *hoo-hoo*, for fear of getting thrashed again if I stayed quiet. I'd quickly realised that it was better to keep up the whimpering in front of them. Amidst all this, Amma saw a man pass by and ran toward him to fall at his feet.

'Panditji! Save us, Maharaj, merciful one! Save my son, mai-baap, my protector! I'll never do it again!'

There was a white *tilak* drawn on the man's dark forehead, and strings of fat prayer beads hung from his hands. His white dhoti and kurta gleamed against his brown skin. I started to whimper louder. He had the face of a good man. As soon as he came over, he asked the boys something in a low voice. Then he turned on Amma, screaming and glaring at her, 'Listen, you damned widow, there's something you've got to understand. This is the village you live in. What's happened to your brains that you can't get it through their heads? These chaps, your nephew and his brat, are not at fault. Do the rules and regulations of this village mean nothing to you?' The man started walking away, rubbing his prayer beads vigorously.

'Don't go, Maharaj! It was a mistake, mai-baap. Forgive us now! It won't happen again.' Amma touched her veil and forehead to the ground and lay herself at his feet.

'You will have to be punished – tell us, are you ready for it?' He sneered through his nose like a whistling black hyena.

'I'll do whatever your grace orders! Save my children's lives!' Amma said through her sobs.

Pointing at Papa, another one said, 'Yeah, your bastard brat swaggers around like a big shot. Filthy widow! Did you give birth to him? Panditji, they're not even hers. They're her widow-licking buddy's. This bastard is Harku's!' He was referring to Dadaji, implying something illicit between my grandfather and his sister-in-law.

'The wise spoke truly, Panditji, you shouldn't trust widows or bulls, they'll fuck anything. And this bastard thinks he can strut around! Sisterfucker threatens to go to court! Catch you in those handy-dandy clothes round here again! Will you ever dare parade about this village after this?' The boy who was reviling Dadaji had been the first to strike Amma with his shoe. Papa remained face-down on the ground, half-dead.

'Fucker gets a big head going to the city! He wants to show off...' one said, rolling up his sleeves.

'He forgot the village rules! This isn't the city, motherfucker. It's the village...the VILLAGE! Here, you live by the rules. Only our law runs here. Do whatever the fuck you can about it.'

'Ah, so this one is Harku's!' The pandit's brow was furrowed. He was glaring at Father's face. Then his expression softened. 'Takes after his old dad. The sod! I kept explaining it to him. Finally had to give up. If only he hadn't been so enchanted with the winds of freedom...' The pandit squatted near Father, balancing on the balls of his feet.

'This one forgot how his father died. The bastard prances down the middle of the village as if he was a chaudhari or something...' someone said.

'Okay, that's enough, tigers! Just let it go now. He'll die. Don't beat him to death. Now get out of here, all of you!' said the black man with the beads. Deep inside, I clutched at a little hope.

'No, no, not like that, Panditji! Punish him so that all the other lowborns think a thousand times before breaking the rules of the village again. Our ancestors worked hard to build all this. Make him lick up his own spittle.' One of them grabbed Father by the hair and jerked his head off the ground, but seeing no movement, he let it drop again.

'Make the bitch lick it up!' He motioned toward Amma.

'What are you looking at, bitch. Spit quick and lick it up, wretched widow!' The pandit was swaying back and forth on his haunches, rolling the rosary in his hand. Amma spat into her palm, then licked it, and everyone started laughing heartily.

'Now tell us, how much money do you have?' the pandit hissed, black as a scorpion, the rosary now around his neck.

'We don't have any money, sir,' Amma started crying again.

He motioned at Father, still prone on the ground, and bellowed, 'Stick your hand in his pocket, bitch. He's brought his wages from the city.' Amma put her hand in the pocket of Father's kurta. When she withdrew it, she had two folded ten-rupee notes in her palm, stamped with the lion seal of the Indian government and splattered with blood. She also held two fifty-paise coins. I knew Papa had set this money aside separately: ten rupees for the bus fare and travel expenses, and eleven rupees for his cousin, Amma's daughter, as was the custom, for having come to eat a meal at her house. The rest of the money he had secured in an inside pocket of his vest when he left home.

'You tramp, no fucking money in his pocket, but he'll dress like a banker! Here, give me ten rupees for the panchayat and eleven for the temple,' the pandit spread his hand out like a cobra's hood. His eyes gleamed looking at the money. His mouth opened like a cobra's basket. His two front teeth were sharp and pointed like the fangs of a black snake. Amma deferentially placed her right hand under her left elbow, as if making an offering to a god, and let the money drop into the pandit's palm; then she fell at his feet. Then they all left. Laughing. Backslapping. The pandit followed, wobbling. From afar you could see patches on the hips of the khaki, police-issue pants of the one who had yanked Father's head up by his hair. The men cast no shadow. There was no sun in the sky. Clouds had gathered. When we were leaving home, it had already seemed like it would rain, but there had been none. All at once, I felt a chill in the breeze. Maybe somewhere far away the sky was crying.

'Papa, it is so lush and green here! Such beautiful fields…and the wells! And the mountains! Our village is so lovely!' I had said this to Father at home as we were about to leave for Amma's daughter's village. I was wearing sky-blue shorts and a new blue shirt. Father had put on a spotlessly white kurta-pyjama. Now it was soaked in red. There were drops of blood on my blue shirt…

'Drink some tea,' she said. I climbed the steps of the well. Placing the tea on the study table, she sat down to write something. Lamplight fell on her left cheek. The fluorescent glow made her dark skin appear white. Maybe she was making notes for the class she would teach tomorrow. Sociology. Social Mobility. Mobility. Social Dynamics. With one hand, I lifted the cup of tea, and with the other, I started to run my fingers through my hair.

There are thirty-six species in the biological family of Canidae. Among them, dogs roam alone. And the dogs and the wolves are enemies. Wolves have much sharper teeth.

An old wound throbbed on my scalp under my hair. *Chhhup… chup…chhhup.* Darkness had spread near the step-well. Dense black.

The gasping of grass. Whispering like hissing black snakes. Steps…
broken and unsteady. One…two…three…fifteen. *Guddup.* 'Kill these
bastards. Not one should be left alive. None.' Hailed by a strident voice,
the entire wedding party came to a halt. A crowd of seventy-five or
eighty demons had gathered and were standing before them. In their
hands were pikes, axes, sickles, and lathis. The wedding entourage was
just departing from the house. Nine or ten old men emerged from inside
with their hands folded and moved toward the group. They had taken
their turbans off and had tucked them humbly under their armpits.
Their heads were held low, down at the level of their shoulders. Their
white hair was unkempt, crushed by the weight of their turbans.

'Forgive him, huzoor, my lord. He's a boy and has always been
stubborn. The crazy boy wouldn't obey even when we tried to reason
with him. We are your subjects, my lord. As long as the sun shines, may
your prestige thrive, mai-baap!'

This was the groom's grandfather. He had placed his turban at the
feet of the bloodthirsty man who was wearing a kurta with its breast-
pocket torn – a triangle of fabric hanging like a half-moon.

A middle-aged man prodded the old man in the stomach with his
staff and said, 'Now forget all this. Did the panchayat not warn you
about riding a horse in the village? You dare do something that no one
has attempted before? Don't you get it, daughterfucker? You've gotten
old, but you're still stupid.' The groom's grandfather did not even lift

his eyes. With his head lowered, the old man said, 'It was a mistake, huzoor. We are your subjects.' His palms were still joined.

'Hey lowborn, you're out to destroy the customs and honour of this village. Has your community not taught you this? You'll be a plague upon the village. We'll see a drought this season. He has broken the traditions of millennia! His sin will taint the village. Such sacrilege in a gujjar village! This is the dark age, *kaliyug*!' All this was said in one breath by one of the village wise men. He was in his traditional attire and looked like a buffoon. On his forehead were painted three religious stripes. In his hand, a string of beads. Across his torso, the sacred thread. On his shoulder, a stole printed with the name of Rama. His chest, bare.

Bhima, still sitting on the ceremonial wedding mare, watched everything in silence. Staring. Smeared with turmeric for the celebration, his face had become even paler. His eyes were wide with fear. Four years younger than me, he was perhaps fourteen.

'You're our master, Maharaj. Don't say such inauspicious things. We'll do whatever you say to atone, Maharaj.' Panic crept across the face of Bhima's grandfather. Hearing the threat of drought, his heart fluttered. A farmer could fight death, but the fear of drought could take his life.

'Nothing can be done now, lowlife. First you sin, then you atone? You did what you had to do. Don't underestimate the consequences.

Atonement for this is beyond you,' said the priest. As he spoke, his eyes glittered at the sight of the bulls tethered outside Bhima's hut. These were the bulls that had been bought with the money Bhima's brother had sent from the city just before summer. He had not yet arrived for the wedding. His wife had lined Bhima's eyes with kohl. Before lining the other eye, she had flirtatiously extracted a promise from him to buy her a nose ring.

'Panditji, you step back. We don't need this bastard to perform any penance,' said a young man, shoving the pandit aside. Irritated, he took a step back, but his gaze did not stray from the bulls. However the glint in his eyes was gone.

'Hey, Nankaya, will you get your grandson off the mare, or should I crack my lathi over his head? I'll make this a funeral procession for this swine of yours!' His eyes bulging, the young man swung his lathi in the air.

'Forgive us, Chaudhari Saheb!' Bhima's grand-father was sprawled at the man's feet. My blood had started to boil. My fists were clenched. I wanted to split the young man's head open with his own lathi. But I didn't have the courage.

'Let's see whose funeral this will be!' A man emerged from the wedding party carrying a lathi and rushed toward the youth. Jostling everyone aside, he was just about to attack. But before he could lift his staff, blows began to rain upon him from every side. I wanted to pick up his lathi that had dropped to the ground, but I couldn't bend down. Women's cries and screams filled the air. The whole sky began to wail. I ran and threw myself on top of the man. Otherwise he would have been killed. A blow landed on my skull, then everything went black, and I lost consciousness.

When I opened my eyes, it was still dark. An oil lamp was burning in the hut. My aunt was sitting near the smouldering stove. The wedding party had left. Bhima had gone on foot. The mare had been returned. Auntie told me all this. My head was throbbing. Someone had tied a piece of old dhoti around it. I don't know when I dozed off again, but a woman's shriek shocked me awake. I made haste to get up, but as soon as I rose, a blow struck my back, and I fell flat on my face. Half outside the hut, half inside.

'Fucking city boy, if you move, I'll unload a bullet in your skull,' someone yelled, tilting my face up with the muzzle of a double-barreled gun pushed into my jaw. To the right, a few feet away, I saw, beneath the white, dhoti-clad bottom of a pale pandit-god, the darkened soles of someone's feet flailing and kicking; swinging on the back of this pale pandit was a fat, snake-like topknot…and another scream. Terrified. Uninterrupted. Splitting the sky in two – *chhann*!

I snapped out of my reverie. A pretty, rainbow-coloured cup had fallen off the table and shattered. The pieces were scattered everywhere.

'What are you thinking about?' She turned and asked without getting up.

I never found out whose black feet those were. The next morning was like every other. The wind was high, just as always. Women went to the well to draw water. Today, they were all silent. Absolutely silent. As if nothing had happened the night before. There was no way of knowing whose life had been snuffed out. When the wedding party returned, everyone went to the police station to make a complaint. The sun was spiritless. Its heat was subdued.

'Get the hell out of here, you bastards. You don't even have any food. We'll take your jewels away. I'll lock you all up right here. I'll throw each and every one of you into hard labour, sisterfuckers! Came all the way to dishonour respectable people!' The sub-inspector shouted, twirling his fat moustache, and everyone retreated. The sub-inspector bawled out to one of his subordinates, who was laughing like a jackal, 'Ramdhani, whose wife was it last night? They say she was really tasty. Lucky bitch, now she's become pure!' I had the urge to smash his head in with a brick that was lying on the ground. The lathi strike from the night before was still throbbing.

That very afternoon, I decided about the future. I would not teach my wife and daughter that a woman's honour can be stolen from her. That she is just a body. They will not become Gargi, the great woman philosopher of the Vedas who was rendered helpless in her questioning. They'll learn the strength of spirit of Ambapali, the Buddha's determined disciple. Their desire for life will be undiminished. They will be able to make the most of their natural qualities.

A scream escaped her. '*Aaaiii!*' I looked at her questioningly. 'A rat,' she said.

'Where could a rat have come from on the fourth floor?' I picked myself off the bed gingerly, so as not to step on the pieces of the broken cup. One by one, I gathered them up, put them in the dustbin, and mopped up the spilled tea. Then I went and stood by the window. Stars were smouldering in the sky. The breeze was cool.

'If you want more tea, I'll make it,' she said.

'No, I'll make it myself. Do you want some?' I was still looking at the stars.

'Half-cup,' came her voice from behind me.

The darkness deepens as the night dies and the day begins to break. Then a single red ray emerges in the vast blue sky. The wolves run, and as they run, they turn into sheep.

Here is the village – our roots, our land. Where there is indignity, abuse, helplessness, and weakness. Every moment, the fear of dishonour. Every second, the feeling of being small. There is sand everywhere, squeezed dry of all moisture. There is no police station for us, no hospital, and no court. There's the village panchayat, but it is not ours. In the panchayat, there is no justice for us, no hearing. Only taunts. In the village, we have no fields. The land was not ours, only the labour. The harvest was theirs, the fields were theirs, the houses were theirs, the earth was theirs. We had just a hut. We had only salt, chilli, and bread to fill half a stomach, and water to fill the other half. But there was no well. We had no new clothes. We had no shoes.

Here in the city, I am an executive in a big government enterprise. An officer. Mr Siddharth Nirmal, Marketing Manager. My wife works as a college lecturer. We have a house. My wife and I have a room, our daughter has a separate room, there is a sitting room for guests, and a study. When our daughter was sick, I called Doctor Punj, a brahmin, to come to our house. He prescribed a good, expensive medicine, and she got better right away. She didn't die of the cold, the way my aunt did. We have a car with an air-conditioner and a middle-aged, Garhwali brahmin driver, Bhatt, who would never forget to bow and greet us when he opens the door. He has never neglected to rush and take my briefcase as I step out of the lift. Our daughter goes to an expensive convent school. Her teacher said once at a parent–teacher meeting, 'Your daughter may be a good singer, sir!' And I called a Bengali music teacher whose name and number I found on the internet. He comes to our home twice a week to teach our daughter music. When our daughter insists, there's McDonald's, Pizza Hut, also Haldiram's. Where we can even fling our money when we pay. We know that even if the money falls, the smiling counter-boy sitting by the computer will be the one saying 'Sorry, sir', in English. We wouldn't even have to express regret. People only offer us smiles in our presence. No one would dare laugh at us. Here there is police. Here there is an expensive lawyer. In this urban world of utter anonymity, there's happiness all around – unending, eternal. This anonymity forever colours our rainbow dreams.

But here in the familiar world, there are the same snakes. The same whispers, the same poison-laced smiles. Our 'quota is fixed'. I got promoted only because of the quota…that's it. Otherwise…otherwise, maybe I'm still dirty. Still lowborn. Like Kishan, the office janitor. Like Kardam, the clerk. Because I'm their caste. His colleagues won't eat food from Kardam's house. He told me this. I couldn't eat with them. Paswan and Kardam ate together, but nobody knew when Kishan ate. Kardam filed a written complaint with General Manager Mahapatra about his fellow-clerk, Gupta. Gupta had called him 'the quota guy'. I even tried to pursue the case. Mahapatra Saheb then called me into his cabin. He discussed the case with me for half an hour. I explained to him how Gupta debased the office atmosphere. 'Mr Siddharth, you are an officer. You shouldn't be prejudiced. Is it because Kardam is also

Scheduled Caste that you…' Mahapatra Saheb narrowed his eyes. 'And it's not as if Gupta used any caste-specific abuse. Kardam has indeed come here through the quota. You know this too. So why does it hurt him? You may go. I'll take care of it.' I saw the same smile on his face that I had seen so often on Gupta's. His decision has been pending for the last five years.

Why do Kardam and Paswan come to see me so often? Why do they tell me their troubles? Why am I the only such officer there? Why does my assistant, Paswan, not hesitate to dispose of my teacup in the absence of my peon, Chedi Khatik? Why don't Gupta and a few others greet me when I come to office? Why does everyone rush to do every bit of work for my deputy, Thapliyal? Is it because of his brahmin surname? Why…why? Are we different? Are we separate from them? Like Muslims? Like Christians? Like blacks? Like those from outside their known turf…are we aliens? Mleccha? Lowly? Untouchable? I was writhing like one of the hundreds of strands of twine Amma's hands used to twist into a rope.

But how clear the stars looked in that village sky. So many! Hanging so low. Climbing on top of each other. Jostling with each other. Leaving no space for each other. Dadaji's saintly words sparkled between those stars. To this day, his sweat sparkles on the harvest's golden sheaf of corn, in the wells, and in the ponds. The fragrance of his hands lingers on the mud walls of that thatched hut. So much is ours. Our earth, our land. Again, I came near the broken steps of the step-well. I started to pluck a water-lily in bloom at the edge. In the starry night, a lily brimming with moonshine.

'What's our plan for the wedding?' I heard her voice behind me. How would she know that it was that very wedding that I thought about constantly? Fear? What fear? Of whom? I walked out onto the balcony. I was looking for a number on my mobile. Deputy Magistrate Shirish Sonkar's name and phone number appeared under 'S' on the screen. He was my junior at university. He is posted in Dausa, Rajasthan. I knew he would jump when he heard my voice. He'd immediately say 'Jai Bhim!' The last time I called him, all he did for two or three minutes was to complain that I never called him, not even by mistake. Even today he would address me as sir. Some people never change. Maybe that's why such relationships never die. Hello, I said as soon as I heard from the other end. But I could only hear a computer-generated female voice saying, 'The number you have dialed does not exist, please check the number you have dialed.' I checked. The number was correct. He must have changed his SIM card.

I came in from the balcony and stood near the big table. 'Siddharth.' I heard a feeble voice. Shom…my friend Shom Sanyal's voice. 'How long are you going to endure this…how long?' Where had Shom gone, I had no idea. His last letter came five years ago, from Jehanabad, in Bihar.

'What are you thinking about? I'm talking to you.' She got up and came close, and wrapping her arms around my waist, asked, 'Have you thought about attending your cousin's wedding? Are we going or not?' She was excited about seeing our village, just like our daughter. She rubbed her dark left cheek slowly against my shoulder, the cheek that a short while ago had seemed white under the neon tube.

The pigeons had long since returned to the ledge. The house was filled with the chirping of their chicks. I pulled the licensed revolver out of the desk drawer and ran my hand over its glossy butt.

'We absolutely have to go. If we don't go, we'll die.' These glittering words emerged from my mouth spontaneously. In the sky, some stars began to burn more brightly.

'What?' She stood gaping at me in astonishment.

Tattoo

'Ufff...these are really old! And faded too!'

This was my first thought, moments after I entered the gym, even before I gathered my bearings. It was like a sudden, heavy downpour. Or as though a door had suddenly opened, and someone had thrown a bucket of water through it without looking to see if there were anyone outside.

Who, then, was now revealed? From whence came this sudden rain, this bucket of water, drenching me so unexpectedly?

As I looked at my battered old shoes, the words 'Namo Buddhaya, Jai Bhim' tattooed on my right forearm caught my eye. The tattoo started slightly above my wrist and ended just below the elbow. A long time ago, my father had had this tattooed on both our arms at a Chhath celebration one year, in our village in Bihar's Gaya district. I was only ten then, studying in the fifth grade at a government primary school in Delhi, where my father worked as a watchman on the government payroll. Back then, such jobs had not been outsourced to contractors.

Oddly, whenever I went to such places as this gym, I always became self-conscious about this tattoo, as I did today about my shoes.

The gym was just about a hundred yards from Khan Market. A grand gym, as ostentatious as the market, shaped like a half-moon and lit by night with all the full moon's lustre. Sujan Singh Park, where resides the renowned author and journalist, Khushwant Singh, lies on one side of the market. On the other is Loknayak Bhavan, an eleven-story building with a jumble of government offices. On the third side is the Ambassador Hotel, reminiscent of colonial times under the British. Finally, on the fourth side is Prithviraj Market, which mostly houses car repair shops, or other small stores that sell everyday necessities. After the grandeur of Khan Market, the lacklustre Prithviraj Market seems as insignificant as a tattered leaf.

The gym was right at the end of Prithviraj Market, at the corner of a service lane. A line of bungalows belonging to government officials and other VIPs started there. This was part of Lutyens' Delhi, maintained by the New Delhi Municipal Corporation, whose billboards exhorted me to 'keep the area clean and tidy' as I parked my scooter outside the compound gate.

There were about twenty cars parked there. A few had drivers, milling around and chatting together. Some were dark-skinned, some wheatish, and one or two had a fair complexion. Among the cars were Accords, Honda Citys, Chevrolets, and Swifts. The cheapest was a Hyundai Santro. Strikingly, there wasn't a single Maruti 800 among them. A poor man's car now relegated to the bottom of the pile.

The matter of the drivers' complexions and the makes of the cars was another thought that sneaked in like a thief through the backdoor of my mind. However, this thought didn't jolt me as much as the first because it was a matter that remained outside the gym door. Out here, we were all the same. Equal. Their cars didn't matter to me, nor did my scooter concern them. It was the vast, sweet ocean of anonymity in which there was not a chance of getting salt in my eyes.

This was the alluring and magical charm of the metropolis. It was intoxicating – and lethal, like Vishnu in the guise of the seductress Mohini…Lethal? My mind hesitated a moment. 'Yes, it's undoubtedly lethal.' But what is to be done? Shaking off an involuntary shiver, my mind slowly recovered. This is why I tease my mind, calling it an amoeba. Even when it is broken to pieces, it assumes a new shape again. Or sometimes, in praise, I call my mind Raktabija, at which it can't contain its joy. My mind doesn't like being called an amoeba. But Raktabija, the demon-king who spawned demons in his own image at every drop spilt of his blood….ufff…that's a name it could kill for. It acquires the stature of an avatar of Raktabija – this fills my mind with pride, making it sway and dance to itself for a while. I suddenly smiled.

'Hello!' a young man seated on a throne-like chair saw my smile and greeted me with one in return.

'Hello!' I answered him readily.

Between me and the youth on the chair was a small rectangular table with a Lenovo laptop and a fat register. His fair-skinned face glowed with the sheen of wealth and bore a long, sharp nose as a mark of his lineage. He wore a blue, branded shirt and had gleaming white Reebok shoes at the end of his outstretched legs. Under the table, my shoes faced his. They had lost their original colour quite some time ago. Only a faint, green tinge remained now. My mind was drawn to them again because of the dazzling glare of his sneakers – 'Really, these are quite shabby and faded.' I drew my feet back and put some distance between us.

The young man got up and stepped forward to shake my hand politely. 'Would you like to sign up?' A gold bracelet dangled on his wrist. At least forty grams, I'd guess.

'Absolutely…' I took his hand, a little hesitantly. 'What are the fees?' He looked about seventeen or eighteen years younger than me. He must have been barely twenty-three or twenty-four. But he thrust his hand forward with such self-assurance that I couldn't stop mine from meeting it. As I put my hand forward, I suddenly remembered my tattoo and, as best I could, turned my arm in such a manner as to hold it downward.

He wasn't paying attention anyway. 'Please have a seat…' He pointed to a chair and sat down himself.

'Thanks,' I said as I seated myself opposite.

'Are you in government service?'

'Why?' His question came as a surprise.

He elaborated: 'Well, we operate under the Corporation's Resident's Welfare Center. They put out a tender, and it goes to those who offer better facilities at lower rates. This is a government employees' neighbourhood, so we offer them a concession.'

I was reassured by his explanation. He didn't find anything out of place in my attire or my manner; he was just asking for business purposes. 'Yes, I am.'

'Sir, the monthly fee is fifteen hundred, and the registration charge is five hundred.' He pulled a form out of a drawer. 'We'll charge you every three months. It's a quarterly fee.'

'That's quite expensive,' I muttered to myself but kept my demeanour such as to suggest that it made no difference to me. My gaze turned to the long gym hall, where three LG split air conditioners were at work.

I had to remonstrate with myself. 'Fifteen hundred rupees? An expense of fifty rupees a day!...No, no...it's not an expense, it's an investment. An investment in my health.'

'Would you like to start today?' His voice was exceedingly gentle.

'Yes, absolutely, I would like to start today, but...anyway who walks around with so much cash nowadays?' I smiled. It felt like a huge expense to incur to maintain my health.

'No matter, sir, we also accept credit cards.' He took a small machine out of the open drawer and set it on the table.

'What do you charge other people?' I couldn't stop from asking.

'It's two thousand per month for them, six thousand for three months; the registration fee is the same.'

'Hmm.' I noticed a young woman on an exercise bike. Her face was blooming with evidence of her high birth. She definitely couldn't be a government servant. In her black Nike shorts, her strong calves and muscular thighs looked attractive and motivated. She paid her surroundings no heed whatsoever. She was in her own world, pedalling the stationary cycle. She wore snazzy sports shoes, but she was too far away for me to see the brand.

On the other side, a middle-aged man and a young girl were walking with long strides on their respective treadmills. The floor of the treadmill was like some kind of road running on electricity. Suddenly the girl increased the speed of her treadmill and started jogging.

'Your name, sir?' he asked, his pen poised over the column on the form.

'Subhash Kumar...' I wanted to add Paswan, but desisted after a moment's thought.

'Is that it, sir? Any surname?' he asked casually. His eyes were still on the form.

'Is it necessary to put down a surname?' Anger suddenly coloured my voice. This was a completely foolish, unjustified reaction. I looked again at my shoes. I had bought them seven years ago. They were quite cheap. I got them for Rs 450 at a Columbus company sale.

'No, sir, it's not necessary.' He smiled. 'Your designation, sir?'

'Under Secretary.' I took the ID card with the Government of India seal from my pocket and placed it on the table with pride. He didn't ask me anything else after this. He filled out all the form's columns with information from the card.

'You've become Under Secretary at quite a young age, sir.' His voice was deferential.

'What do you mean young? I am forty-plus.' I thought of the assistant who had joined service with me and had only made it to the rank of Section Officer. But even this could happen only because of reserved places in promotion; otherwise, those in higher positions would have made us run around in circles. Why can't our people manage to land unreserved posts even today?

'Forty-plus…really sir? You look around thirty.' He was flattering me, but friends too had often told me the same.

'What's your name, brother?' My self-confidence had grown as we discussed my age and rank.

'Rahul Upadhyay!' He answered softly. 'You may call me Rahul, sir.'

'Okay, I will, Rahulji – after all, you are my trainer.' I laughed, and he smiled too.

Then he took my credit card, swiped it in the groove of the machine, and deducted the amount. After a moment, the machine spat out two slips. Rahul gave me one and attached the other to the form after taking my signature.

'Sir, first go and run slowly around the lawn to warm your body up.

Afterwards, do ten minutes of cycling.' Rahul motioned toward a vacant cycle, next to the young woman.

I exited the gym hall. It was warm and humid outside. It was the 5th of July, but so far there had been no sign of the monsoon. I hadn't felt the heat fifteen minutes earlier, when I had come to the gym. Maybe the chill of the air-conditioning had made the air outside seem more oppressive. I started walking slowly and at the same time inspected the premises. The compound had a big gate onto the road, along which several patrons had parked their cars. Extensive lawns flanked both sides of the entrance. A path had been laid down around the perimeter, and I was now walking on it. A Ford Endeavour was parked behind the gym. I picked up pace and started to run. My breathing became heavy. Then I went back inside.

'Now do the cycling,' Rahul said as he saw me.

The young woman was still cycling. I made every effort not to look at her muscular calves, but I got a peek a few times anyway. I started cycling alongside her. She got off after a couple of minutes and disappeared. As she left, I thought again of the shoes. Had she noticed them? Because they were so old, their green had become quite faded and dingy. In one place, some of the stitching had come undone.

'Have you ever exercised before?' Rahul came and stood by my side.

'A long time ago.'

'Where?'

'Here in Delhi,' I said and went quiet. What could I tell him? That I used to exercise in the J.J. Colony park in Nangloi, where dogs, goats, and even pigs often perform their own gymnastics? However Rahul didn't ask anything further.

'Whose Ford Endeavour is that behind the gym?' I was trying to change the subject because often conversations that start with 'Where do you live' and 'What's your surname' ultimately end with the inevitable – caste. I was always trying to avoid arriving at that point.

'It's mine, sir. I live in Madhu Vihar.'

'Very good. Your own car, your own house!' I smiled.

'No, sir. I don't have a house of my own yet. I rent my flat for twenty thousand rupees a month.'

'Oh, that expensive?'

'Yes sir. Rates have skyrocketed since the arrival of the Metro... Everyone's Punjabi in our apartment block.'

I could see he was heading in the same direction again. I turned my attention to my shoes once more.

'Are you also Punjabi, sir?' he asked, most inconsequentially. 'Here we go!' I muttered to myself. I didn't answer. I figured he was trying to get at it in a roundabout way.

'Sir, you use 'Kumar' for a surname, don't you? That's why I asked. Many people in our apartment block use this surname too.' He smiled and walked away.

There seemed to be something behind his smile. But there was nothing I could do about it. Then I asked myself why I was always so guarded, so vulnerable, and so aggressive when it came to caste distinction.

I returned home but couldn't shake off my unease. I told my wife and children about it. My daughter suggested I put Cherry Blossom black liquid dye on my shoes to hide the real colour, so they'd look new. My son said I should buy a new pair. I preferred my daughter's advice. 'That's thrifty,' I said, pretending to agree in their presence. But the truth was I didn't want to change the shoes. I wanted to prove that they were still serviceable.

I went out for a walk after dinner and bought two bottles of dye. I got busy that very night, and after an hour's hard work, the shoes were turned black.

'They'll dry by tomorrow,' I thought and went to bed.

When I awoke the next morning, my first thought was of the shoes. I got up and went straight to the verandah. I touched the shoes and found them still wet. When I returned that evening, I saw the shoes had dried, but there was no gleam to them. I took an old cloth and started to shine them, rubbing vigorously. Then I thought of shoe polish. I applied shoeshine with a brush for ten minutes, but the soles were still light green. Seeing me thus engaged, my wife said, 'Take them to the cobbler, he'll give them a good shine for ten rupees.'

I put the shoes in a polythene bag and went to the cobbler's stand. He wasn't there. A vegetable seller nearby said that he'd left at six. I looked at my watch; it was seven. I shouldn't have come to a cobbler to get my shoes shined anyway. Rather, I should buy an expensive polish from the Woodland showroom in the market and try that. I walked to Woodland and bought the costliest black polish I could find. I wasn't in the mood to go to the gym, but I talked myself into it anyway.

'Hello sir,' Rahul greeted me as soon as I entered.

I smiled too and said hello. 'What should I start with today?'

'First, do ten minutes of cycling, followed by ten minutes on the treadmill at a brisk pace.'

I sat on the cycle and started to pedal. As each pedal rose, I looked at my shoes and told myself that no one else was paying them any attention; everyone was absorbed in their own exercise. Putting everything else out of my mind, I started cycling. I then did a brisk walk on the treadmill for ten minutes.

I was a little tired from twenty minutes of continuous exercise. I sat down on a bench at whose head was a long bar holding several heavy iron plates. I lifted my foot and rested it on my thigh. I found this relaxing, but suddenly my anxiety reared its head again – my shoe was now in everyone's line of sight! I immediately put my foot down.

After that, Rahul had me do the butterfly exercise, and it really wore me out. I returned home before my hour was up.

The next day, I decided to first polish the shoes thoroughly and change their colour, and go to office only after lunch.

'The sole will lose its original colour only after two or three rounds of polish,' I told myself and applied two further layers. The old colour was there still, though faintly. But yes, there was something new about the shoes now.

In the evening, I was back at the gym. Even after cycling, the treadmill, and the butterfly exercise, I wasn't feeling tired today.

'Little by little, you'll build up stamina, sir,' Rahul explained when I told him.

'What's new?'

'Sir, today let's do a thigh exercise.' I then lay on an incline above which there hung several heavy weights that you had to lift with your feet. He first demonstrated it to me and then told me to do it.

'Good, sir.' He encouraged me when he saw me doing it right.

'He must surely be looking at my shoes, there's still some green on the soles.' Each time I lifted the heavy plates, my shoes caught my eye and grated on my nerves. I reasoned with myself about the futility of my worry.

'Different colour, sir!' A boy, seventeen or eighteen years old, exercising on a bench press nearby, said smiling as he looked at my shoes.

'Bastard...' I muttered inwardly. However, in the next few moments,

I composed myself again. 'No, he doesn't mean to be sarcastic. He's just a boy, and he must have said it just to tease me or to strike up a chat.' I calmed myself and made no reply. 'Being reserved is the greatest strength of all,' I told myself and felt quite reassured.

A few more days passed like this, but I now felt apprehensive of someone commenting on my shoes each moment of every hour I spent in the gym. Finally, to be free of this, I took myself in hand – this is it! I should neither hide them nor be ashamed of them, I told myself firmly, and found unprecedented joy and strength in the thought. I was now doing every kind of exercise and had yet to be questioned by anyone. The best support is to make oneself strong from within.

I had come to accept my shoes.

After fifteen days of daily workouts, my health and, what's more, my self-confidence began to improve.

'Sir, do the bench press today, this will make your chest muscles strong,' Rahul advised, after having me do a half-hour of exercise.

'Will it be alright at my age?' I asked doubtfully.

'Absolutely, sir.'

'Let it be, brother, I don't want another worry. What if I get a pain in my chest?'

'Not to worry, sir. Your chest will expand – you've got a slouch.'

'Are you sure? What if I end up being forced to rest and have to go on leave?' I wanted to puncture his enthusiasm.

'Don't you worry. I'll get you started with some light weights. Now, go ahead and lie down on the bench.'

Just as I was going to lie down, my mobile rang. Vir Singh Jatav's name was flashing on the screen. He was a colleague from another ministry. Our offices were in the same building, and we held the same rank. 'Jai Bhim, Jatav Saheb!' I said in response to the 'Jai Bhim' he greeted me with. Talking on the phone, I walked out of the gym. We spoke for a brief while. When I finished, I turned to find Rahul standing behind me. 'Okay, so he heard me saying Jai Bhim. Well, I don't care about it anyway.' I said to myself.

'Sir, you're a Jai-Bhim-wala too?' Rahul came close to me and whispered.

'Certainly…' I was emboldened by his saying 'too'.

'Sir, I'm Rahul Valmiki…my grandfather had changed my father's surname, saying it is Buddhist. I am a Buddhist, sir.' He pulled out a locket hanging hidden inside his shirt and showed it to me. It bore a small figure of Lord Buddha. 'My grandfather was a fourth-class employee in the Delhi police, and my father retired as sub-inspector in the same service.'

'Nice to meet you here.' I shook his hand. My eyes went once again to the gold bracelet around his wrist. And to his fair skin and high nose. Finally, I turned to his gleaming white shoes. 'This one has changed his shoes,' I thought as I looked at my own dyed ones.

Suddenly, my eyes fell upon the tattoo on my wrist: 'Namo Buddhaya, Jai Bhim'. Ufff, these old and discoloured shoes can always be changed, but this tattoo? It has seeped, drop by little drop, into my consciousness and has permeated my entire being. 'Oh! This tattoo!'

Hello Premchand

When the gentleman rushed over to me, he was panting. I knit my brows and creased my forehead as I tried to place him. He understood my confusion.

'Perhaps you don't recognise me?' he asked.

'No...I mean, yes...I mean that you look like Premchandji to me, but this is impossible. This is 2006. It was only recently that a cruel American ruler mercilessly executed Saddam Hussein...this is something the world, even with its short-term memory, hasn't forgotten yet...and just a short while ago, a dalit neighbourhood in Gohana was burned to the ground in broad daylight...and what's more...in exchange for salt, adivasi women had to trade those intimate moments which the middle class mentality calls honour...those women called it force...not just this, high caste politicians ditched the Congress 'hand' to fall at the feet of the woman riding the 'elephant' of Bahujan politics...for all these reasons, it's no less than a miracle.'

'No, you're right. I'm not Premchand.' His face betrayed anxiety.

'So who are you?'

He pulled something out of his bag. 'Just listen to this sentence: "Whatever else may change in this world, bhangis will always remain bhangis. It is tough to make them human." What do you think?' he asked.

'Did you say this?' There was irritation in my voice, or derision, or maybe it was just dissatisfaction.

'A thakur character in Premchand's story "Doodh ka Daam", The Price of Milk, says it.' Then he stared at me quietly. He started to crack his knuckles. Despair, as if born out of days of turmoil, showed on his forehead. He thrust both his hands into the pockets of his kurta, and when he pulled them out again, the linings of his empty pockets dangled like the wrung-out teats of a goat.

'Why would he have said such a thing? This is my concern.' The words tumbled out of his mouth after a long pause. At the same time, he pulled out a sheaf of rolled-up papers from his bag.

'That was the first story, and this is the response…yes, and please take this too.' As he said this, he pulled a coin from his bag. It was a silver coin dated 1936, bearing the image of a smiling Queen Victoria sporting a crown.

'I know you can't use this any longer, but you'll fetch a price for the value of the old silver. The papers have gotten old, please have them typed.'

So this is this story's backstory…Typing now: *tak tak tak…*

Light had not yet appeared in the distant sky, but the clatter of the day had already begun in the small hut. Mai took some water from a pot in the corner, gargled, and splashed her face. After washing herself, she picked up her broom, opened the door, and stepped outside. It was still dark. As soon as she opened the door, Tommy began to flounce about at Mai's feet, whining. He was wagging his tail with such energy that his waist began to swing along with it. Still whining, Tommy began to bark in a peculiar way as though he were saying in dog language, 'Eh, Bhungi Mai, go on and get my roti.'

There was no hostility in this barking, as there would be toward a stranger. Rather, there was fawning and complaining. As he barked, Tommy sprawled at Mai's feet, and sometimes he pressed two of his paws to the ground, arched his back, and sprang up in the air.

'I'll get it for you, just wait a minute,' Mai said, understanding his entreaty, and went back into the hut. She moved aside the cloth covering a wicker basket, took one of the two rotis she'd kept there, and put it in front of Tommy.

'Here, eat your fill.' She lovingly put her hand on his head and poured a little milk on the roti. The milk spread over the plate and started to soften the bread.

'It's all thanks to the grace of the Thakur's wife.' Tommy looked at Mai with moist, black eyes. In the middle of his dark brown fur, a streak of white spread across his throat.

'Eat up now,' Mai scolded, seeing that he wasn't eating. He stood there whining, then started to bark and went outside.

'Mangal, get yourself to school on time, son.' Mai ruffled Mangal's hair with her hand.

'Oh, and there's a roti for you in the basket, eat it! Don't go to school hungry.' Mai heaved herself up with her hands on her knees. She wasn't very old – she may have been around thirty – but after Gumad Kaka had died, it was as though she had aged in just a year or two. Everyone thought that Mai would move in with someone else. Either it was her deep attachment to Kaka, or her concern for Mangal's future – Mai hadn't married again.

'My Mangal will get an education and will find work in an office. He'll never make a living doing dirty work…why should he do work that denies him dignity?' Mai was forever mumbling. Even now, as she got up, she muttered these words like a mantra.

When Mai left, Mangal got up to close the door, but he stopped, hesitating. He saw that the roti was left untouched in the plate…this meant that Tommy had gone to see Mai off and would return to eat his roti in peace only after she had left.

A weak light now leaked through the sky. Mangal stepped outside and picked up the neem twig lying in a niche of the wall and started to brush his teeth. It was Mai's strict order that he clean his teeth every day. A few years ago, a severe toothache had bothered him one night. Since then he hadn't had another. Eventually he started to like the tooth-cleaning ritual and he'd started to bathe daily too. This didn't cost anything. He snapped a neem twig from a neighbourhood tree. Ever since the government had laid piped water in the neighbourhood, there had been no water scarcity.

A few years ago, there had been no such conveniences. Had there been, it would have been so much better. His aunt, Gangi Chachi, wouldn't have been beaten in the middle of the village for drawing clean water from the Thakur's well. The village panchayat, perched on their platform and impelled by divine authority, had handed down the punishment of a shoe-beating for Gangi Chachi. The entire village watched silently. That evening, Mangal witnessed the Thakur's 'righteousness'. He still couldn't forget the face the Thakur revealed that night.

'Mai, you fed Suresh with your milk. Why didn't you save Chachi from that bloody Maheshnath?' Mangal asked Mai.

In the backyard of the Thakur Saheb's bungalow, with a cloth tied over her mouth and nose, Mai was shoveling the Thakur's family shit into an iron bucket with an iron rake. Mai motioned at Mangal to back away, but he refused. Seeing that he wouldn't budge, Mai finally scolded him, 'Arrey! Back off, or you'll get spattered!'

Mangal left then, but that night he pressed her again.

'Why do such questions even occur to you?' Mai enveloped him in her lap and showered him with affection.

'Tell me, no, Mai, couldn't the Thakur have given Chachi one pitcher of water...he pretends to be a good man.' Mangal caressed Mai's chin with his little fingers, and Mai's eyes filled with tears.

'We're untouchable, son. The Thakur has to uphold tradition and demonstrate his valour.'

'So, when his son drank your milk, we weren't untouchable, but we became untouchable when it came to water?' Mangal said, rolling his eyes. 'He got fat drinking my share of milk.'

'We're servants, son...we're reared on pity. It's because of the value of my milk that Gangi and Jokhu were spared, otherwise they would have been killed,' Mai spoke in a mutter, like someone having a fit.

'Servants don't have any rights, only duties. And the Bhungis and Gangis were born to be servants...' Mai was suddenly quiet, and though Mangal asked her many more questions she gave no answers that night. She just kept repeating, 'You should never have to do this work...you should never have to do this work.'

Brushing his teeth, Mangal put a bucket under the tap. '*Kukdu kuu...*' Dhakad Chacha's fighting cock hopped up on to the wooden beam of a hut and crowed. This cock would always win for Dhakad Chacha in cockfights. All around was the cool air of the morning and the chirping of birds. No one else had come down to the tap yet, so Mangal took the opportunity to bathe right there.

Today he used two bucketfuls of water. He was about to bathe with the third, but just then Santo Chachi chided him, 'Don't waste water, dear...spare some for others.' Mangal picked up his full bucket and returned to the hut. Mangal wasn't little any more, he could carry a full bucket of water.

When Mangal went into the hut and saw Tommy engrossed in

chewing on his roti, his thoughts turned to mischief. 'Here, let's give you a cold water bath.' He put the bucket on the ground and, cupping some water in his palms, he threw it at Tommy. Some of the water fell on Tommy and some on the floor. Tommy jumped up right away, retreated to one side, and started to bark angrily at Mangal as though saying in dog language: 'It's not nice to joke around with someone who's eating.'

'Okay, okay, don't get so uppity, go ahead and eat your roti.' Mangal waved him back, then took his roti, sat down next to Tommy, and started to eat.

When it was time for school, Mangal arrived on time, as ever. Seeing his clean shirt and shorts, headmaster Sevanand Arya made him stand at the head of the assembly during prayer – just like he did every day. He presented him as an example to be followed.

'Mangal, never abandon your studies, son. One day you'll make it big.' Sevanand Arya patted him on the back. He recognised Mangal's sharp intelligence clearly. Sevanand Arya used to be Sevasingh Yadav, but after becoming an Arya Samaji, he changed his name and attitude. Many in the village did not approve of his behaviour toward Mangal. One day, some of the fathers complained to the Thakur. Thakur Maheshnath summoned Sevanand and said, 'Masterji, pay attention to the education of the other boys in the village as well.' Then the conversation veered toward the education of Maheshnath's son and daughter, Suresh and Divya.

Mangal also frequented Sevanand's house. Sevanand's wife Kamlesh Devi was even more progressive than Sevanand. Mangal and Sevanand's daughter Vipin Kumari were playmates.

'Girl with a boy's name, old spinster dame.' When Mangal teased her, she sulked. But sometimes she became distraught and complained to her mother, 'Ma, Mangal is teasing me! He says that I have a boy's name.'

'No, a name isn't anyone's property. Take the word 'agni' – if you add a 'dev', it is a man's name, and if you put 'devi', it's a woman's… you are both my daughter and my son.' Kamlesh Devi stroked Vipin's head lovingly. 'Now you'll never be afraid of any man or woman…fear no one but yourself.'

The days flew by like a hawk that soars through the sky without flapping its wings. In no time, Mangal was in eighth grade. He had developed such a taste for reading autobiographies and life stories that he had devoured all the books in the school library. He also read the autobiographies that Sevanand Arya had at home. Among these, he read Omprakash Valmiki's *Joothan*, Surajpal Chauhan's *Tiraskrit*, and Roop Narayan Sonkar's *Nagphani*.

Sevanand was surprised by Mangal's reading beyond his years, but deep inside he also found this reassuring.

'Have you read B.R. Jatav's *Meri Safar aur Meri Manzil*?' Sevanand asked Mangal one day, and Mangal nodded.

He asked another question. 'What kind of ins-piration do you get from all these autobiographies and life stories?' Vipin was sitting next to him.

'Determination, Maatsaab, that you should never let your circum-stances defeat you.' Mangal's eyes were lowered.

The day the eighth grade results were out, Mai came home in the afternoon with a high fever. Mangal was placed first, but seeing how bad Mai's health was, he couldn't feel happy. Mai kept muttering until nightfall, 'You don't worry, I'm not going to die now. I still have to get you educated, get you married, feed your children.' She feverishly repeated this over and over again, all night long.

In the morning, Mai opened her eyes right at the time she went to work every day. 'Mangaaaal...' a faint moan issued from her throat. Mangal was in deep sleep. He'd stayed awake all night changing the compress on Mai's head. He had drifted off at some point. Tommy heard Mai's voice and gazed at her intently.

'Go get Mangal,' Mai said, and Tommy walked over to Mangal and began licking his face to wake him up.

'Mai, you're okay, aren't you?' Mangal held a glass of water to her lips. Mai's forehead was still hot. She had shat and pissed herself; she had no strength to get up.

'Mangal, my child...I'm going.' As she said this, tears began to flow from the corners of her eyes.

'Don't talk like that Mai...how will I live without you?' Mangal burst into tears.

'You'll have to be brave...how else...' Mai said in a tired voice.

'Don't quit your studies...and don't ever take up this work...I don't want my son to have to carry piss and shit...' Mai was repeating this over and over.

'You relax, I'll get some water.' Mangal soaked the compress in water and placed it on Mai's forehead. He lifted the bucket and stepped outside. Tommy stayed at Mai's feet.

'What use is work that denies you honour,' Mai muttered in a trembling voice. When Mangal returned with the water, Mai was sleeping peacefully. Mangal only realised a while later that Mai was dead. Even Tommy had not barked to announce her death. For want of medicine, Mai had died of an ordinary fever. The news swept over the village like a whirlwind. Mai was, after all, a famous wet-nurse.

'Malik...' Mangal had arrived at the bungalow. Thakur Maheshnath was talking to some people in his drawing room. Outside, Suresh was teasing Mangal.

'Here, take this!' Maheshnath threw five hundred rupees toward Mangal.

'Do the funeral rites and, from tomorrow, you come in her place,' Maheshnath said, and turned once again to his conversation. It was considered a sign of the Thakur's largesse that

Mangal had been allowed unchecked as far as the drawing room.

Mangal bent down and gathered the rupees. He took the money and headed straight to Dhakad Chacha's place.

'Chacha, the Thakur gave five hundred rupees for Mai's funeral.' Mangal pressed the money into his hand. Dhakad was also of the bhangi caste, but he'd learned wrestling and was also the head of the community. He was the disciple of a Muslim wrestler.

'Five hundred won't get you anything, son...you need more than that for the shroud and everything...but don't you worry, we'll all get together and do something.' Dhakad Chacha made it sound easy, but anxiety clouded his eyes. People in the community did not have much to get by on – their pots and pans rang empty.

'Should I ask Headmaster Saheb, Chacha?' Mangal tried to assuage his concern.

'Let's see!' It was as though Dhakad Chacha had seen a way out of the labyrinth. 'I'll see what I can do.'

'I'll be right back.' Saying this, Mangal hurried toward Sevanand Arya's house. It wasn't yet eleven o'clock, but the sun had started raining down fire. Mangal was running, galloping, barefoot, when he recognised a familiar bark behind him. He turned to see that Tommy was running after him, along with another dog, Jabra. Tommy and Jabra were very close. When Mangal was at school, Tommy and Jabra kept each other company – playing, jumping, and wrestling.

'Where are you running off to, Mangal dear?' came Ghisu's voice, as he lay stretching his limbs under a nearby banyan tree.

'I'm going to Maatsaab's house, Baba,' Mangal said as he ran.

'Hey, listen, come over here.' It was now Madhav who sat up and waved him over. Mangal came running and stood under the cool shade of the tree. He told them everything in a subdued voice.

'Here, son, take this money. What better purpose could it serve?' Ghisu pulled out eighty rupees from his pocket and thrust it into Mangal's shirt pocket.

'All this is due to the good fortune Budhiya has brought... every inch of the house has flourished since her arrival.' When Ghisu praised his daughter-in-law, a proud smile bloomed on Madhav's dark face as well.

'Here son, have another fifty.' Madhav took out fifty rupees from his pant pocket and gave it to Mangal.

'In times of mourning, even strangers become our own. After all, we're part of one village family.'

'You go home and arrange for the shroud and the rest...we'll come along with four or five more men...there's no need to involve Maatsaab,' suggested Ghisu, and Mangal returned home.

Dhakad Chacha had also collected money from the houses in the neighbourhood – ten, twenty or fifty rupees – from whomever he met. He'd also gathered all the things required for the cremation. A few neighbourhood women bathed Mai for the last time. Outside, Ghisu, Madhav, and a dozen or so men had gathered. Together they formed Mai's funeral procession.

After the last rites, people slowly began to leave. Mangal was left all alone in this big world. A short while ago, with so many people standing by him, he'd forgotten his loneliness and grief. Now the desolate night seemed fearsome to him.

Man's greatest fear and despair is loneliness, and the night accentuates the pain and alienation of this loneliness. But how could he blame them…they had their own troubles, their own families, how long could they stand by him? Life is lived on its terms and with courage. Mangal began to miss Mai terribly.

'Tommy, if you weren't here with me, I don't know what I'd do.' He hugged Tommy, and suddenly he began to hiccup and a stream of tears rolled down his face. He hadn't felt orphaned when his father died, but now with Mai's death, he was at once truly an orphan.

The days ahead gaped menacingly at Mangal. The teeth of the phantom of Mangal's future were so bloodthirsty that his heart caught in his throat. He managed to get by for a couple of weeks on the money left over, but soon his pockets emptied. Then a daily summons came from the Thakur's place: 'Come to work now or the job will be given to someone else.' Mangal knew well that many a mouth watered at the prospect of finding work at the Thakur's place. If he refused, they would be delighted. After all, there was no other house where you got as many leftovers in exchange for work. A hungry Mangal thought that there was no fire bigger than the one in the belly. At least at the Thakur's he would get roti twice a day, and perhaps he could even continue with his studies. But first he should take care of his stomach. How long could others feed him? And who knows if they fed him only so that they could grab the job at the Thakur's. He remembered the milk, cream, sweets, and the ghee-smeared rotis at the Thakur's house. All his resolve started to crack. 'I can only study if I survive.' But just as he tried to go to work, Mai appeared to block his way: 'Mangal, my child, don't ever pick up the broom and the basket...this is a quagmire that looks like firm ground, but in reality it is no ground at all.'

Finally, exhausted, he went one day to see Sevanand Arya and told him everything. In fact, Sevanand had noticed Mangal's deteriorating condition over several days. But like a good teacher, he was quietly waiting to see if Mangal could find a way out.

'You've studied enough, now go ahead and pick up your broom and basket.' Sevanand, who was sharpening a pencil, watched Mangal's reaction surreptitiously. 'Maheshnath is absolutely right when he says "What good is education to the sweeper's son – it's not as if he's going to become a collector."'

'But what about Mai's last wish, Maatsaab?' Mangal's voice

quivered, and tears glittered in his eyes, but he composed himself.

'Mai is dead, now who is there to hold you to her wishes? If you don't work, how will you eat?' Sevanand kept sharpening his pencil.

Mangal fell into deep thought, 'How will you eat? How will you eat?' The question pounded against his brain like a sledgehammer.

'Where should I go then, Maatsaab…what should I do?…I want to study…Even if I don't study, I'll die…Study or not, I'll die of hunger anyway.' Having said this, Mangal finally broke down. A deathly silence spread through the room.

'Mangal…' The voice of Kamlesh Devi, who was sitting with Sevanand, broke the silence. 'Why don't you take a month off somehow, and something will come up.' Kamlesh Devi's encouragement was like a straw to the drowning Mangal.

'Why don't you get him admission in Delhi?' asked Kamlesh Devi, seeing reassurance on Sevanand's face. 'In Dayanand Anglo Vedic School.'

'Yes, this is a good idea, our friend Pandit Ghasi-ramji is there as well.' Sevanand Arya reassuringly kept sharpening his pencil.

'These days he's in the management committee, he'll also arrange something for his room and board.' There was excitement in Kamlesh Devi's voice.

'But how will I take a month off…Thakur Saheb is sending orders every day…I…I don't want to pick up the broom, ma'am,' Mangal said in a wretched voice.

'Then tell him you are sick, son,' Kamlesh Devi showed him an escape route. 'The grief over the loss of your mother is no small matter.'

Mangal headed back toward his hut from Headmaster Sevanand's house with a weary heart and heavy steps. The setting sun had started to fade, and the road was empty. He was emerging from under a pipal tree when a crow knocked him on the head as it took flight. He immediately became anxious. Mai used to say it was a bad omen to be struck by a crow.

'What luck have I got left that I should fear losing...oh, it's all nonsense. His nest must be up in the tree,' he consoled himself. As he walked on he saw Halku and Devidin from a nearby village coming toward him. Ever since Halku's land was sold, he'd been a labourer in Zamindar Maheshnath Thakur's fields.

'Mangal...Thakur Saheb has asked you to report for duty tomorrow morning for sure,' said Halku as he approached Mangal. 'It's been more than a fortnight since your mother died.'

'But I don't feel good, Kaka,' Mangal said in a forlorn voice.

'But, child, Thakur Saheb will not accept this...you'd better understand. He just won't accept...' Halku abruptly stopped mid-sentence. 'And I can't afford to ignore his order, my life depends on the wage he gives me...and not just mine, I've got four other mouths to feed.' Despite his helplessness, Halku seemed to threaten Mangal.

Devidin, who until then had stood by listening silently, burst out.

'Arrey, why are you threatening the child, Halku? His mother has just died…Is he a thakur or a demon who doesn't feel another's grief and distress?' Devidin's sense of justice and his rebellious nature wouldn't allow him to stay quiet. It was this spirit that made him lose two sturdy sons to a civil rights struggle.

'So tell me, Devidin, what am I to do? Where do I go? If I catch him, I give up my soul, and if I don't, I give up my life.'

'Come Mangal, stay at my place. My wife will grumble for a while, but then she'll yield…she's not bad at heart. She anyway has no one left now.' Devidin alleviated Halku's anxiety, but his voice was heavy with the memory of his two grown-up boys.

'Devidin bhai, you're a khatik and he's…' Halku said as if to remind him.

'I know.' Devidin cut him off. 'Halku, you think I don't know? His mother raised your zamindar's boy on her milk…I know everything. For me, everyone is equal. With skin and flesh as one, who is shudra and who is brahmin? Sadguru Maharaj Kabir taught us long ago, but we remain ignorant.'

Mangal looked back and forth between Devidin, whom he didn't know, and Halku, whom he knew well. He was wondering why Devidin was helping him even though he was a stranger.

'Come on, son, be a cane to this blind man!' Devidin stroked Mangal's head.

'Brother, what will I tell the Thakur...do tell me,' Halku sounded worried.

Devidin paused briefly, and then suggested, 'Tell him anything, my good man...say that the young fellow just ran away.'

'When the boy doesn't even want to do the work, why is the Thakur so obsessed about it?' he muttered.

Mangal thought to himself that he must somehow survive the month and then think about the future. This was a tremendous relief for him. A helpless, destitute man doesn't get swept away in plans of long-term profit. He chooses the path that offers hope for immediate benefit because there are many obstacles on the path to long-term success, obstacles that he has already faced. Mangal found refuge in Devidin at a very opportune time.

Mangal was happy at Devidin's house. He found Amma to be just like Mai. She was good to Mangal. In exchange for meals full of ghee, milk, yogurt, and fresh vegetables, he did the accounts every morning, and washed the vegetables for Amma's stand. As they grew older, this laborious work had become more difficult for them, but life had to go on. If the old couple didn't earn anything, what would they eat? A whole month went by in a whirl.

'Baba, Headmaster Saheb has made arrangements for my further studies in Delhi.' One evening Mangal told Devidin about his plans. Devidin listened to it all solemnly. 'I didn't want to leave without telling you and Amma.'

'We've become very attached to you, my dear. Our heart aches at your going...the old woman had said just a few days ago that little Mangal has large eyes like our younger son did.' Then Devidin restrained his emotions. 'But we shouldn't hinder your progress with small-mindedness.' Devidin took him to Sevanand Arya's house under cover of darkness, so no one would see them.

Sevanand handed Mangal a letter addressed to Pandit Ghasiram, and told him that they had already discussed his case over the phone.

'However much anyone asks your caste, don't tell them...you heard me? To no one!' Kamlesh Devi put so much emphasis on 'no one' that a question sprang up in Mangal's eyes.

'What if they insist?' Mangal asked innocently.

'Say you're yadav.' There was despair on Sevanand's face, stirred by the immutability of a heartless system.

'Things still haven't changed...but surely they'll change by 2036... we'll see.' It wasn't clear if Sevanand was comforting Mangal or himself.

It was the end of June when Mangal, with a few rupees in his pocket, headed alone to Delhi.

When time treads on the wet earth, it leaves no marks. Days, weeks, months and years went by. In the meantime, Vipin Kumari became a doctor, got married, and had two children. First Kamlesh Devi passed away, and then a little later, Sevanand Arya. With Pandit Ghasiram's financial support and his own indefatigable efforts, Mangal was selected one day for the Indian Administrative Service. He did so on merit too. Because he hadn't revealed his caste, he had never made use of a reserved place.

Mangal was now Mangal Das.

'This is my own village.' Mangal Das spread out the map of the district and circled his village with a pencil. He had come to the district as collector. All of his old acquaintances were gone.

Mangal Das had been in public service seven or eight years, but he was still unmarried. Everyone in Mangal Das's office made fun of the Collector Saheb's bachelorhood in his mid-thirties. But no one ever saw Mangal Das laugh. He had a strict temperament in matters of administration as well.

When news reached Vipin Kumari that Mangal Das had come to the district as collector, she went straight to his office to meet him. She gave her card to Mangal Das' personal assistant. When the PA buzzed Mangal Das on the intercom, the answer came: 'Please wait ten minutes.'

Mangal's behaviour came as a shock to Vipin. Various thoughts buzzed in her mind. 'Ensconced in his position, has Mangal become like other officers?'

'Please come inside, madam,' the PA said, bowing with extreme politeness. About eight to ten people left the office just as Vipin arrived at the door. The assistant held the door open. Vipin Kumari had only taken a few steps forward when she saw a magnificent-looking man standing with his hands folded.

'Is this the same Mangal?' Vipin thought to herself. She hadn't seen him for about twelve years.

'You! I mean…I…you are…Oh-ho, I am sorry.'

Who knows if Vipin Kumari was dazzled by the splendour in the room or was dazed by Mangal's changed appearance – she couldn't speak for several moments.

'It's me, Mangal, Vipin! This is just a mirage of material comfort.' Mangal recognised Vipin's surprise.

The two spent some time catching up. She also told Mangal about the troubles with her job transfer. Then she left. A few days later, Vipin was transferred to the same place where her husband was working.

'Now why don't you get married?' Vipin Kumari asked one night after dinner. Over the next few meetings, the old ease between them had returned. Meanwhile, she'd visited Mangal's house several times with her husband Dr Dinesh Yadav, and their children.

'Yes, Das Saheb, Vipin is right,' Dr Yadav echoed.

'Why, are my peace and happiness bothering you?' Mangal Das said in his deep voice, and they both burst out laughing. Seeing them laugh heartily, Mangal Das also smiled.

'Oh yeah, Dinesh, I forgot…those days Mangal was completely infatuated with Divya,' Vipin exclaimed, clapping her hands.

'Who's Divya?' Dinesh said with curiosity, seeing the colour rise on Mangal's cheeks.

'How do you know, liar?' Mangal Das looked embarrassed. 'When did I ever tell you this?'

'These things are never said, one just hears them. And you did say something, don't you remember? You said Divya was so beautiful, so tender.' There was certainty in Vipin's voice. 'Tell me, don't you remember saying that?'

'I have no idea. When did I say it?'

'Arrey bhai, let me in on this…who's this Divya?' Dinesh sprang forward and sat upright on the sofa.

'Arrey Divya…Divya Singh, our village thakur Maheshnath's daughter, Suresh's sister, the same Suresh who used to come to you to get free asthma medicine for his mother,' Vipin clarified. 'Did you hear the news about him, Mangal?'

'What?' Curiosity bloomed on Mangal's face.

'About the Thakur Saheb.'

'What about the Thakur Saheb? Stop speaking in riddles.' Mangal Das sounded impatient.

'Maheshnath's cousin Durganath took him to court. Durganath's son had become a big shot in the secret service in Delhi. From there he put together such a case that Maheshnath was left flailing. Soon everything was seized, and the scoundrel was left with nothing.' Vipin Kumari was enthusiastic.

'Oh, that's terrible!' A cry escaped Mangal's mouth.

'Terrible? It's great! He was a tyrant...he had earned the curses of so many. Mangal, if prayer can turn a stone into a god, a curse can also break a stone...and he was merely an idol made of flesh and bone. They say in the end he died a horrible death. He didn't even have strength to get up, and there wasn't any money in his pocket for his bare necessities.' Vipin characteristically badmouthed the Thakur while she kept her eye on Mangal. 'What good does arrogance do? Everything is fleeting.'

'What is Suresh doing?' Mangal Das was inquisitive.

'No news of him here. But three or four years ago, he left for Delhi...he became a security guard in some private company there. He wasn't educated. He failed his tenth class board exam three times and finally gave up his studies. He was a big, tall fellow so he found a job as a guard.'

'I want to visit the village some day, and it would be great if you could come along.' Mangal wanted to ask about Divya, but instead he asked, 'Is there news of anyone else?'

'Yes, the son of Madhav Bhaiya and Budhiya Babhi became a teacher in the primary school.' Vipin was making the conversation meander on purpose. 'These days, he's become involved with

Ambedkarji...Bhaiya and Bhabhi tell him to get married, but he says he is married to the cause.'

'Anyone else?'

'Yes, nowadays Dhakad Chacha is working with an NGO on a campaign against manual scavenging.'

'This is wonderful, I will definitely help them...our lot won't be improved until this disgraceful practice is eliminated.' Mangal Das' tone was businesslike. 'And?'

Mangal Das' 'Ands' were never-ending, but Vipin Kumari wasn't going to give in too easily either.

'Okay, brother, we should leave now. There'll be no end to this chit-chat with you.' Vipin stood up to go. 'Look, Chunmun has already dozed off, and soon it will be Nikhil's turn.'

'What about Divya?' Mangal Das couldn't stop himself after all.

'Divya is still in the village with her Ma. They got her educated till BA, and have kept her home since. She did okay in her studies, but there was the same old issue of thakur honour. 'Our daughter won't go to work.' They'll just sit there high and mighty, twirling their moustaches, even as the rats rattle the empty vessels of the house. What is the point of such false majesty? But yes, now I understand why bandits are always thakurs in the movies. Living off a salary is a disgrace for them. Suresh did well, choosing a life of labour when he became a guard.' Vipin Kumari said in a taunting tone.

'Divya should work,' Dr Dinesh Yadav said, his hands on the car's steering wheel. 'Otherwise, what's the point of being educated... squandering the state's money.'

'Yes, but...well, I have to tell you, Mangal, she liked you too. She was always praising you. After all, you were the school's most intelligent student.'

'Really?' Mangal Das' eyes widened. The old image of Divya Singh shone in his big black eyes.

Vipin and Dinesh left. Mangal returned to the room and sank into the couch. 'You won't understand, Vipin – once you become the master, it's difficult to sit with the servants. One's own thinking and societal pressures put a person in this dilemma. These societies have been bound by the cycle of master–servant rituals for thousands of years. They will take time to break. This tradition or habit will not die easily.' Outside, there was a horrid heat, and inside, the chill of the air conditioner. Mangal slipped off his shoes and stretched his legs out on the table in front of him.

'Mai...look Mai, I didn't pick up the broom and basket...' Mangal grabbed Mai's shawl and was running after her...Mai kept walking... 'Mai why don't you say anything?'...Mai stopped...'Now you should get married...I'll die only after I see my grandchildren'...'But whom do I marry?'...'Divya'...'How could I ask her Mai?'...'Why should you ask...look, the Thakur's wife has herself come to offer her daughter's

hand in marriage'...'This is a strange proposal, what should I say?'...
Mai was muttering...'But what should I do? I was a servant and what
chance does a servant have?'...'Now you must ride to our door on a
horse, Mangal Singhji. You're the ruler now, and we your subjects....'
Suresh has come too, in his blue security-guard uniform. 'First you be
my horse, then I'll marry your sister.' But Suresh refused to turn into
a horse until Ghisu, Madhav, Devidin, Halku, and Budhiya all came
together, encircled him, and made him a horse by force...Mangal
became a ten-year-old and climbed onto his back...'Let's go, horsey,
tik tik tik...Suresh is my horse...Suresh is my horse...Mai! Look here,
I didn't ever pick up the broom and the basket...'

'Saheb, why don't you have some milk?' Moteram Shastri's voice
woke him up with a clatter. It took him a few moments to realise where
he was. Moteram Shastri stood in front of him clutching a glass of milk.

'What happened, saheb?' Moteram Shastri handed him the glass.

'Nothing. Perhaps some hidden desires have become dreams and
come to haunt me in my loneliness,' Mangal Das said and took the
glass. 'Moteram, your children are studying, aren't they?'

'Which one should I send to school? There's not just one, I have
five sitting on my head: Agluram Shastri, Baniram Shastri, Chediram
Shastri, Bhavaniram Shastri, and finally Phenkuram Shastri.' Moteram
Shastri shook his head and left.

'It's good if such desires remain dreams...there is no truth, no dream larger than society...I should get them some work...that would be a real help.' IAS officer Mangal Das was thinking like a master.

The next morning, Mangal Das's convoy was heading toward the village where his roots lay, where Divya Singh, who was also dreaming her own dreams of freedom, was.

And now the typing is finished...

It was a strange coincidence that as I finished typing, I met the gentleman again that same evening. This time he wasn't alone. There was another gentleman with him who looked just like Dr Ambedkar.

'You recognise me?' As soon as he came close, the gentleman fired off the question, 'Is the typing done?' I nodded, but several questions flashed in my eyes.

'This great man is Dr Ambedkar. Surely, you must recognise him?' The gentleman said, introducing the man next to him.

'Babasaheb!' I lurched forward and grabbed his hand.

'Here, read this!' he stopped for a moment. He pulled a packet of fifteen or so pages from his blue coat and handed it to me. It was on fancy paper, stitched together.

'After reading several of Premchandji's stories, I drew some conclusions. In 1941, I gave this speech at the annual meeting of the Bombay Municipal Worker's Union. Keep it, read it at leisure,' he said, seeing me flip through the pages. But by then, some of the lines were knocking on my brain: 'You do not seem to realise the tremendous power you have in your hands. You can, simply by refusing to work, spread more havoc and disaster in a week than Hindu–Muslim riots should do in three months.'

'You've made a very good point,' I put my finger on these lines.

'You have to read this with the story...this is the placenta and the umbilical cord. These come out at birth along with the child.' The gentleman who looked like Premchand patted my shoulders. Come, let's together sing the national anthem of Independent India. He took my hand and walked ahead.

The three of us stood together at attention: '*Jana gana mana adhinaayaka jaya hey, bhaarata bhaagya vidhaataa...*'

Scream

'Crime is very seductive. And revenge a trickster,' came Father's voice – drifting, breaking – like logs in a mountain river. 'You must not fight with the Patel's son.'

She had almost screamed, her eyes filled with the astonishment of orgasm.

'You really are a devil,' breathed the forty-something Mrs Deshmukh. Her makeup caked on her face. 'I'm going to ask that son-of-a-bitch Suneja…where he's been hiding such a fabulous treasure until now.' Then she drifted off. I wanted suddenly to give her a powerful kick, but instead I only prodded her lightly with my foot.

'Wait…wait…I'm tired.' The words dribbled out of her mouth effortlessly when she felt the nudge, like shit flows when you have diarrhoea. My mouth filled with spit.

My village was very beautiful. It bordered three different states. Across the mountains lay Gadchiroli in Maharashtra, and to the south was the town of Chandrupatiya in Andhra Pradesh. The people of the village had no idea what an administrative district was. Father used to come over to our village on the mountain. He's the one who told us that our village was part of Dantewada district, in Madhya Pradesh. Chhattisgarh wasn't a state then. Father explained that you would pass Chandrapur in Maharashtra before arriving at Jagdalpur in Madhya Pradesh. The villages on this side of the mountain were in Dantewada, and those on the other side were in Gadchiroli. On the far side of the river was Chandrupatiya. Our village, Bhinsa, was on the mountain and was made up of fifty houses. Papa did several jobs. He butchered and skinned animals, harvested honey from beehives, made toddy, and even laboured on the landlord's fields at the base of the mountain. Ma had died a long time ago, and I could hardly remember her face.

I never saw Papa arrive on time at the fields. Everyone else was always on time. The Patel hurled abuses, 'Petura, you goddamn loafer… you're late again!' To his face, Papa sang the Patel's praises, and then crouched under a charpoy and smoked a bidi. After a while, when the Patel left, father started to make fun of him.

'Fucking Bajirao, haven't had a shit again today…only one big fart… *bhwooon*!' Papa made the sound with his mouth, and everyone laughed aloud. He unwound his dhoti, lifted his foot, and mimicked the Patel. 'This is our land! Who is the Patel to order us around?' But soon he started working alongside everyone else in the fields.

Bajirao was the head not only of our village temple but also of several others nearby. When he marked his forehead with religious stripes, he looked terrifying. I had even seen him rape the junior priest's wife. The junior priest was lighting the evening prayer lamps. His wife had gone to the defecation ground. I saw her pleading. But the Patel didn't let her go. In the vast, empty ground, her scream was stifled by his panting.

I attended Father's school. The school was near the church. Tenth grade. I studied English and could speak it a little.

'Work hard, and you'll be a big man one day. Study as much as you can.' I was very influenced by Father. 'Learn English. A man can become great only if he knows English. By all means, serve your mother tongue too, but only English makes a man a lion.' I learned only much later that Dr Ambedkar had taught the very same thing. I studied all night by the light of a small oil lamp.

It was almost time for the tenth grade exams. The school was far, two kilometres away. I walked down the mountain. On the way, I had to pass through a small forest – our forest, our land. When school was over, I headed home, dilly-dallying. Dinkha always came with me. Only Dinkha and I went to school from our village. Dinkha was in ninth grade. That day, he hadn't come. School was over. I set out for home. Without Dinkha, the road seemed deserted. Every day, we talked as we walked together, so we never paid attention to the time. But today, the road seemed very long. Unending.

It was late afternoon by the time I reached the forest. You could see the mountain up ahead.

'Hey, you! Stop…where are you running off to, Kristaan?' The Patel's son, Vinayak, was sitting on a fat, bent-over tree branch with a few other boys from the village.

'I'm not a Christian, malik.' I kept walking.

'Hey, who told you to go anywhere? You've got some balls...get over here.' Vinayak jumped off the branch, and came and stood in front of me.

'Show me your bag. What did you steal?' He grabbed my satchel and dumped my notebooks on the ground.

'Malik, give them back...they'll be ruined...Father will be angry,' I pleaded.

'Your pants are really great. Where did you steal them from?' He grabbed the back of my pants and let out a loud laugh. All his buddies started laughing too.

'Father gave them to me, malik...please, they'll rip,' I said as I jerked my pants out of his grip.

'What else does your Father give you?' He winked at his buddies, and they started laughing again. 'Okay, hand them over,' he said with dramatic flourish. I held my pants tighter. 'Take them off.' They all held me down and started prodding me with their fingers.

'Malik, I'm not wearing any underwear,' I entreated him with my hands folded. After this, all five of them fell on me, ripped my pants off, and flung them into the dust.

'Fantastic...so this bastard's been cut!' They were left gaping. Their eyes popped. Awe over my genitals shone in their bugged-out eyes.

Moments later, they started signaling each other with their eyes. Four of them pushed me roughly face-down on the ground. I could feel the breath of the Patel's son in my ear. I could hear the sound of drums coming from my village in the distance…*dhap-dhap-dhap, gud-gud-gud, pad-pad-pad.* Over there, my people were playing the drums. Guntiya, one of Vinayak's friends, jerked my head up and punched me hard on the nose. I screamed with as much ferocity as I could, but my scream was swallowed by the woods. I fainted. When I came to, I heard Vinayak's voice, 'Your turn, Guntiya.'

'No,' came Guntiya's voice.

'Then kick him in the rear.' At this, a strong kick landed on my backside. 'Now we've cracked his big club.' *Dhap-dhap-dhap, guddar-guddar-guddar, pad-pad-paddar*…the sound of drumming could still be heard from the village. They were leaving. My people were playing the drums and drinking toddy.

I hobbled home. It was as if the whole world were jeering at me. I couldn't even tell anyone. But if someone looked at me, it felt as if they knew everything. I wanted to die, but somehow I couldn't do even that.

A few days later, exams started. I couldn't go back to school after this, but I did take my exams. The days just slid by. My results came, and I passed. But I hadn't scored very high marks, and Father was very disappointed. The year before, in ninth grade, I had got the highest marks. He kept asking me questions about what had happened. What could I say?

'I don't want to stay here any longer, Father – please send me somewhere else.' I pestered Father over and over, and he was worried. Finally he gave me a letter and an address. He put me on a bus from Chandrapur to Nagpur. On that letter was the name of the principal of a missionary school there.

I arrived in the afternoon. I had stayed awake throughout the overnight trip. It was the rainy season, and when I got down at the bus terminus, it was drizzling. I went to the school and handed the letter to Father Samuel. He placed me in the eleventh grade without any objection. I don't know what was in the letter, but when Father Samuel read it, he smiled and looked up at me. I had not opened the letter; the thought had never even occurred to me. But when he smiled, I wondered for a moment if Father had mentioned what had happened. They found me a room in the hostel and gave me clothes to wear. They made arrangements for me to eat in the mess. Time spread gauzy curtains over my memories, and they became unclear. I passed twelfth grade at the top of my class and entered college to study sociology.

This was a different world altogether. The other boys had no cares in the world. They lived for today. They didn't care for tomorrow. There were some mahar boys, and they formed their own group. Most of them didn't accept me as one of them. They called me 'Kristaan', just like the upper caste boys. When we did actually talk, the first question the mahars asked was whether I was SC or ST. Then they asked my subcaste. And then they turned their backs. But the upper caste boys turned away as soon as they heard I was Scheduled Caste. The attitude of the teachers was the same. A few of the mang–mahar boys were still friendly to me.

One day in anthropology class, Kulkarni Sir was lecturing on human races. When he came to the Negro race, he looked directly at me and said, 'You! Stand up.' He pointed at me, smiled and said, 'Look, here is the Negro race. Thick lips, wide nose, prominent brow, round skull. But with more height.' All the students burst out laughing. Everyone but the dalit students, who couldn't laugh. Most of them looked just like me. Kulkarni Sir also laughed aloud. As he laughed, he squeezed his beady eyes shut. 'Yellowish skin, a small, flat nose, a cramped forehead...just like the Mongolian race, a descendent of Genghis Khan...a blessing from the languor of the trip from Mongolia to Maharashtra,' I thought as I watched him laugh. The bell rang. Kulkarni Sir left.

The upper caste girls were ogling me. There was a strange fervour in their eyes. A lustful hatred. I thought of Papa. He was short and had a long nose. His lips were thin and red. He had a high forehead. Mai was tall and thin. She had a wide nose and thick lips. The beauty they had both endowed me with was ugliness, and that ugliness was both my beauty and my strength. Ugliness too is beauty; I had seen such a transformation. Differently beautiful.

I was in my second year when I stopped receiving the scholarship from Father. He had come to Nagpur to meet me, and when he told me to adopt the path of Jesus, I hedged. Religion no longer appealed to me. All religions seemed to wear the same guise. Father didn't have any interest in anything beyond God and religion. Ultimately he said, 'I am helpless in giving you a scholarship against the will of the church. May God bless you.' I had already anticipated this. I was indebted to him. It was only because of his kindness that I had gotten this far. But did religion hold any meaning for me? More than religion, I needed bread and dignity. My uncle Paul had become a pastor, but the village pandits still called him the son of a matang. I thought it better to remain unclaimed terrain than to be known by some strange name.

I liked Jesus. And Father was even more beautiful to me than Jesus. Father's calm eyes would drink up all the anxiety in my heart. I could lose myself in him like a stream that merges into the river. But I found the church haunting. Utterly bleak and forlorn. There was no life there. There was no rapture or celebration. The church bell struck fear into the silence. There was no quiet serenity there like there was in the village temple. In the temple, there was life and enthusiasm, and joy. But we were still segregated from the temple's deity and festivity. Like the mahars and the mangs, we couldn't touch them either.

Even before Father's final letter arrived, I was offering lessons and was earning enough to get by. In the meantime, I completed my BA and moved to Mumbai. I enrolled in a postgraduate program at the university. I struck up a friendship with another student, and together we rented a small room in a tenement house. A few months passed like this. My money was running out. I asked everyone I met for work. Three girls lived together in Room 2: Sharda, Padmini, and Revati. Three brahmin girls from Ratnagiri. Tall, extremely fair, blue-eyed girls. Just like English girls. I had read somewhere that the Europeans in Maharashtra had first landed at the Ratnagiri port, from where they had then fanned out. The girls also studied in college. And at night, they danced in a bar. It was Sharda who arranged part-time work for me in a massage parlour.

'Work here until you find some other job. You can quit then,' she patted my shoulder without inhibitions. 'Cash in your pocket will come in handy in good times and bad.' As I was desperate, I started work at the parlour. I couldn't find tuition jobs here like I had in Nagpur. I had studied science through twelfth grade. But to continue with science wasn't possible without money. This is why I took up sociology. When I worked as a tutor, people enquired about my qualifications. In the massage parlour, I worked from 4 p.m. to 10 p.m., and made a hundred rupees per shift. This was no small change. It was significantly more than what I needed. And yet money is never enough because aspiration is always in excess of it.

Life started getting better immediately. I loved the uninhibited vibe of Mumbai. Here no one asked about anyone else's caste. I could breathe freely in this world. A new freshness filled my lungs. The joys of the city. I wanted to forget Vinayak by any means possible. But his memory followed me like a ghost. Maybe I was addicted to digging up the graves of the past. I found a few students. But I made a lot more money, and in a lot less time, at the massage parlour. I couldn't rely on the tuition money. Most often, people didn't pay. I had to make the rounds for months. Even then the money came in piecemeal, and this amounted to nothing. There was no question of credit at the place where I bought my provisions. The material world had no room for excuses. For this reason, I wasn't very keen on tuition.

I was in college from morning until two in the afternoon. From there, I headed home. Sharda, Padmini, and Revati also returned by then. As soon as I arrived, I put the rice to boil on the stove, changed my clothes, and washed my face and hands. Sometimes Sharda invited me over to her place. The girls were very well-mannered, as I learned during my time with them. Sharda would always put out a full spread to go with the rice – pickle, papad, daal, and vegetables. That day she had laid everything out as usual, but her face was ravaged by sadness.

'Are you ill?' I asked.

'Seems like it. I skipped college today.' A mist of sadness filled her eyes.

'You need medicine. C'mon, I'll take you,' I said as I ate. I was trying to speak to her in her Bombay Hindi. If a man tries, what is it that isn't possible?

'No, man, I'll be fine. No worries,' she said in a sad voice. 'I really miss my Ma.' As she said this, she undid two buttons of her T-shirt. Underneath, her black bra flashed on her pale skin.

'How's work?' She put some rice on her plate.

'Fine.' My glance fell upon a faint scar on her chest. 'What happened there?'

'Oh, nothing! A customer burned me with his cigarette.' She covered it gently.

'You, Revati, and Padmini are all related, right?' I especially wanted to know about Revati. I liked Revati a lot. Very tall and utterly fair. Her eyes were melancholy, her face small and triangular. Her sadness was not reflected in her face, though. She was a radiant beauty. And yet, though I didn't know why, Revati sometimes screamed horrifically. She screamed like an animal being slaughtered. She had been raped. A relative of hers had done it when she was twelve or thirteen. Sharda told me about all this one day, much later. Padmini was also tall and fair, but I wasn't attracted to her. I sensed a strange kind of motherliness in Sharda. She stood apart. There was splendour in Revati's complexion.

'No, Padmini's from my village. Revati's from a neighbouring one. We just met here. I came to Padmini. Revati was already here. From the same caste, you know.' She was rolling the rice over in her mouth. As soon as she started talking about caste, I went quiet. I assumed that now she would ask about my caste too. My mind started racing to think of what I would say. I couldn't say I was brahmin – this carried the danger of being caught. Patel? I had the height for it. No, it wasn't right to hide my identity. I wasn't here to marry them! If they wouldn't feed me, so be it. I was hardly starving. I prepared myself mentally, but she didn't ask me anything.

'Were you dancing with a customer?' I looked at her burn scar.

'You're so naive.' She covered it carefully with her T-shirt. 'I like your sincerity, but it won't help you here. You've got to get smart. This is no village, it's the city.' She smiled. Behind Sharda's, Padmini's, and Revati's smiles and heavily made-up faces was a stifled shriek I was only just beginning to hear. It was just like someone who tries to scream while she is being strangled.

I had been working at the parlour for only a few months, but the head of the parlour, Mr Suneja, had begun to trust me a lot. He was Punjabi, and clearly very professional. Perhaps my standing had grown because I spoke fluent English. He acknowledged this several times. I changed my name to Tyson. This was an occupational necessity. I was never dishonest in my work. When honesty is the policy, then there is profit in dishonesty. But after testing me several times, Suneja was reassured.

I started to learn the business. The city quietly taught me a great deal as well. Suneja started to send me to the homes of exclusive customers. Sometimes even to give massages to women. Fat women left alone in big bungalows with fearsome dogs. They were mostly Marwari, Madrasi, and Punjabi. Some Maharashtrians too. If I went often enough, they started to recognise me. Even their fearsome dogs stopped barking. They would wag their tails when I arrived. Did they feel some affinity to me?

This is how I met him. He was a Malayali. Everyone called him Pillai. It was December, and the intoxication of a slight chill had begun to spread across Mumbai. I arrived at his hotel room at three in the afternoon. I rang the bell. When the door opened, there stood a fortyish man wrapped in a white lungi. 'Suneja…' I had only said this much when he moved to one side with an effeminate gesture and said, 'Come, come…Sit, I'll be right back.' He headed toward the bathroom. From behind him, I stared at his ridiculous gait. He moved like Revati. There were several pictures on the table. They were of him in various dance poses. I recognised him even in heavy makeup.

'You're…' The photos were now in my hands.

'Yes, yes, I'm a dance teacher…I teach dance to film actresses.' He had a South Indian accent. He cracked his knuckles elegantly. I was once again reminded of Revati.

He lay face-down on the bed. I massaged him quietly. Suddenly he got up and started to kiss me roughly. I didn't understand what was happening but threw him back on the bed with all my strength.

'No...no, I'll pay extra.'

I started to pack my things.

'One minute.' He turned and went to the cupboard, then placed three bundles of hundred-rupee notes in my hand. 'Take this. I'll give you more.' I still couldn't figure out what he wanted. But as soon as he stuffed the wads of cash in my hand, he made an obscene gesture, and I understood. I had never seen so much money except in films. I could take revenge on Vinayak. I could send the money to the village. I could pay off my debt to Father. I could buy Revati a dress, and most importantly, I could settle my university expenses for the whole year.

Face-down on the bed, Pillai looked just like the Patel's son, Vinayak. I heard the distant sound of drumming. *Dham dham dham dhama dham.* The tambourine was playing. There was the mountain, the forest spread out before it. I was racing through the jungle like a savage beast.

'Don't tell Suneja...here is payment for your hard work.' He winked. So this was work. Labour...For the first time I understood that labour had many meanings in the city. The very thing that made me want to die back in the village was considered 'work' here. And one got paid for it. Here, labour had value. This opened up a new world. This new face of the city was a revelation for me. Three days later, Pillai returned to the massage parlour. 'If you need anything get in touch.' As he was leaving, he gave me Mrs Deshmukh's number and a letter. From the third day, I had plenty of money. But was this the beginning of the end – the third day after death when the soul departs the body? I couldn't have sensed it then.

A week later it was the Christmas holidays. I hadn't gone to see Mrs Deshmukh. I didn't have any business with her. I had more than enough money for my studies. I missed Papa a lot, Father even more. When I was in Nagpur, Father brought me news every couple of months of Papa and the village. But after coming to Mumbai, I hadn't been able to get any news of them. It occurred to me, one day, that I had no idea if they were even alive. Before heading home, I bought a few expensive bottles of liquor for both Papa and Father, and several sets of clothes for Papa. When Papa saw me, he went crazy with happiness. He took me immediately to Baba's dwelling on the top of the mountain to pay my respects. I had been visiting Baba Dhujnath here since my childhood. He never went anywhere.

Papa gave one bottle of liquor to Baba. Chasing off a goat, Baba said, 'Petura, I won't take this bottle.' Then he called out to his goat and looked at me, 'Come back, son.' The goat came back. 'Petura, you know, don't you, that if you keep on spending money, you'll exhaust even King Kubera's treasure. So your son has brought home his earnings.' Baba was addressing Papa but kept looking at me. 'If the tree does not draw water from the earth, it dries up and falls. A man should spend his wealth wisely.' There was determination in Baba's dry, forlorn eyes. 'Come see me tomorrow,' Baba said to me when we were leaving. 'A hungry soul shouldn't eat poison. Come on, come here.' We could hear Baba's voice behind us, stopping the goat from munching leaves. Was Baba actually saying all this to the goat?

I couldn't gather the courage to go and meet Baba again. I knew that Baba hadn't been talking to the goat, but to me. All the way home, Papa recounted stories of Baba's spiritual powers. We bow our heads in fear of the power of what we cannot understand. Both God and Mumbai's dons cause fear in the same way. Baba wasn't like this; he was full of love. But sometimes love also causes fear. It was his love that terrified me. Sometimes when we stand before a great man, fear consumes us. This was why I couldn't go see Baba again.

Father had taught me the power of education, and the city had taught me the power of money. The intoxication of money prohibited me from thinking about anything else. After returning from Mumbai, the village seemed like a wasteland. I ran into the Patel's son, Vinayak, on the road. But perhaps he had come intentionally. There was a fat gold chain around my neck. Gold rings sparkled on my fingers. Vinayak couldn't speak. He couldn't even smile. Next to me, he seemed like a beggar. I saw the defeat in his eyes. Then I came back to the city. My heart wasn't in the village. I wanted to earn more money. I wanted to see Vinayak absolutely crushed. Only the city would do. Somewhere along the way, studying had become secondary.

I met Mrs Deshmukh. She was a cunning woman. She counted every penny. She had risen from dire poverty, she told me. Mr Deshmukh was twenty-five years older than she. She wasn't his wife, but she had been shrewd. She had transferred millions of Mr Deshmukh's wealth to her name. This shrewdness had taught her that you shouldn't trust anyone. I felt pity whenever I saw her. When we destroy someone's trust, perhaps we destroy our own first of all. Mrs Deshmukh had destroyed her trust in herself. Just looking at her, I knew that she had become very lonely and insecure. Before destroying someone else's trust, shouldn't we consider a hundred times how it will affect us? But Padmini called this savvy. She regarded this as a necessity of the city, and therefore thought me a fool. Even though she never said it, the pity in her eyes made it clear.

Mr Deshmukh couldn't get around any longer. Even the first time I went to their house, he just sat there, unmoving. If he hadn't blinked, I might have thought he was a corpse. A living statue. His breathing was so shallow that his chest didn't even stir. Yet, just two years ago, he'd had women in every city in the country...perhaps even abroad. So said Mrs Deshmukh.

One day, Mrs Deshmukh embraced me right in front of him. Mr Deshmukh's presence made me despair. He was an old man. 'Like this?' Showing Mr Deshmukh, she took my penis in her palm and lifted it up as though she were about to throw a spear. Mr Deshmukh's eyes suddenly opened wide and then closed. Two teardrops leaked silently from the corner of one. Mrs Deshmukh saw this too. I saw a blissful peace on her face at that moment – the peace, the sanctity of revenge. I had always perceived just such a spiritual peace on Baba's face as well. She paid me more that day. I took the money without a word, but could not silence the questions in my eyes. Perhaps she had read them inscribed in my gaze. 'Because you were my accomplice in revenge,' she said.

Mr Deshmukh was still there. Eyes closed like a solitary statue. 'You shouldn't make anyone your own against their will…understand?!' she screamed at Mr Deshmukh. This was a strange mystery. I had questions to ask, but the rules of my profession prevented me. Mr Deshmukh had opened his eyes when he heard this. I was the first his gaze caught. Surprisingly, there was no hatred for me in those eyes. Rather, there was a kind of kinship, like that between travellers of the same road. Then his eyes fixed on Mrs Deshmukh. He became utterly helpless, like an unarmed combatant face-to-face with his enemy. There was surrender in his eyes, a desire to be free from anguish, while Mrs Deshmukh's eyes were glittering like a wild animal's. A spiritual solace relaxed her brow.

Life was schooling me quickly. Walking the path that we call sin gives us a better and fuller understanding of life. Is the goal of being sinless something we attain only by walking in sin? Do all the beatified arrive there by traveling these same roads? Had Mr Deshmukh transcended love and hate? Would Mrs Deshmukh eventually arrive at the same place? What would happen to me? These questions kept pounding on my consciousness.

The roads I had taken served to make me smarter, but I would always remember Papa. I thought of Father. I would also remember Baba and his goat: 'No one eats poison because they're hungry.' But I had begun to understand indisputably that the road to power was not straight. It is winding, rugged, and full of ravines. I had to conquer it by my own firm resolve.

Mrs Deshmukh kept me in her house on a monthly salary. This was even more convenient for me. I found more time for my studies. Vela was also concerned about my schoolwork. At her insistence, I started to call her Vela instead of Mrs Deshmukh. She said her name was Velamma. She wasn't from Maharashtra, but from Andhra Pradesh. 'I'm starting to fall in love with you,' she often told me. It seemed to me that even she didn't believe these words. Their true import had long since faded for her. So, in order to make herself believe them, she repeated them over and over. I could always read the exhaustion and despondency of these belaboured efforts in her face. It occurred to me that she was describing her love to a toy like a stubborn child would.

If there was anything besides this stubbornness, it was loneliness and the feeling of a void. She just wanted to fill this emptiness with me. But she was always cautious regarding money, and this caution didn't allow her to trust anyone.

'If you were a little older, I would marry you,' she told me when Mr Deshmukh had only been dead ten minutes. His body was laid out on the bed. The statue had changed its posture. The doctor said, 'He is no more,' and left.

Time carried away the days, weeks, and months like a cat that pounces stealthily on half-dead mice. Meanwhile, two major events occurred. First, I completed the first year of my MA in first division; second, I cleared the preliminary civil service exam. I remembered Father who always said that education is a great strength. Along with authority and money, it becomes a great power. Living in the city had taught me this. The uncertainty of the future also kept me on my toes. That was when I met her.

Someone had given a party at Vela's house. She came to the party that afternoon. She must have been twenty-one or twenty-two. I sized up her sari-swathed body just like Papa would squeeze a goat's thigh and estimated its weight. My professional experience had taught me all this. At these parties, my job was to deliver drunk women to their cars or to their beds. Vela wouldn't ask anyone else to do this. She kept me by her side and wouldn't leave me even for a moment – the same way she guarded all her property.

'She is the wife of Varun, the Deputy Commissioner of Police.' Vela had caught me looking at her. 'He'll shoot you.' I didn't know then that these words were conceived in the womb of the future. Hearing the word 'police', I became very uneasy. But later, unforeseen circumstances led me to drop her to her home. The police car she had come in broke down. Varun wasn't in town. Vela sent me with strict instructions that I shouldn't utter a word to her the whole way.

I found her so attractive that I forgot Vela's warning. She said her name was Shuchita. Then she was quiet. 'I'm from Jabalpur,' she said. Then she fell silent again. Between her words and her silences, I kept looking at her chin. Her full, plump chin. I looked at her nostrils that flared like a petulant child's. The same sadness rested on her brow that Revati had in her eyes. She seemed like a copy of Revati. Revati wasn't mine. She didn't belong to anyone. She had committed suicide. She had believed the riddles of rebirth preached by quacks. This belief had swallowed her.

Revati had succumbed to the sorrows of life. I wish she could have fought. Was Shuchita preparing to kill herself like Revati? Her extinguished eyes ignited questions in my mind. Sad people seemed suicidal to me. But I wanted to save her. I wanted to tell her that life isn't just sadness, nor is it just happiness – it is both, and maybe neither. Life is perhaps nothing more than a prop to go on living. Maybe she knew something about my relationship with Vela, or maybe my appearance repulsed her. She was extremely quiet. Yet that afternoon, on the way back from dropping her home, I had no idea that this contempt and hatred would turn into curiosity, and that would eventually draw her toward me.

Ugliness then became beauty unmatched. The sharpest weapon of all. Do women place more importance on a man's power, and his disrepute amongst women, than they do on his beauty? Do women strip more quickly for notorious men? Is contempt too an invisible step toward attachment? Did scholars of the theory of *rasa* believe that the colour of *sringara* was black because of our black skin and manly strength? Why do the white castes still believe the colour of erotic love to be black? The women abducted by Indra – were they not our women, whose dirges are recorded in the Rig Veda? Could those women not abandon their old infatuation with colour, long after their abduction? I saw myself flailing like a tiny insect in a web of questions. In my heart, all I wanted to do was spit at the hollow pandits and their scriptures. Shuchita, Vela, Revati…all of them were just bodies to me.

Then she started to meet me. She made Vela the pretext. I was very eager to meet her. Although she took the initiative, she didn't display any enthusiasm. Was she bound by the doctrine of need? After a few encounters, her attitude began to change. She saw her own reflection in me. What could she be missing, I wondered. Maybe her man was impotent – my think-ing was that of any normal, young guy. Finally, one day, despite trying to hold it back, the question burst out. We were two bodies burning in a single furnace.

She had also done a BA in sociology. Then, like most Indian girls, her mother and father had got her married. They took a dip in the Ganga to atone for the sin of their birthing a daughter. She was a girl from a lower middle class family. In DCP Varun's caste, girls as beautiful as Shuchita were scarce. Because she bore the surname Sharma, I assumed she was brahmin. But she didn't think of herself as one. She told me after a few meetings, 'We're a different kind of brahmin.' There was no embarrassment on her face, only scorn. 'Brahmins don't consider us brahmin. But what can we do? After all, brahmins are the role model here.' That day, I thought of my college friend Girish Shukla. He had suggested that I take a brahmin surname. That would change my colour, my ugliness, my language, my behaviour...all my characteris-tics. That surname would give me strength. But my conscience couldn't stand for this. Girish Shukla, even though a Shukla, still worked as a waiter in a hotel. His father was a power-loom mechanic in a mill. Did being a Shukla mask his poverty and his abasement? I saw more purpose in being a rich untouchable than a poor brahmin. I had to make my own people strong so that patels couldn't commit atrocities against them, so that mahars and khatiks would be friendly to them.

Varun wasn't ready for this wedding. He had rejected his father's decision outright. Then his mother urged him on like a well-trained pet. She spoke of the honour of his father and the community; she threatened to die. 'If you want to carry on with someone on the side, by all means do; but you have to marry this girl.' Varun agreed. He acceded to both his mother's propositions. Shuchita told her story in parts.

'Compared to you, Varun is very weak.' I understood what she was implying. 'Vela has often told stories of your strength.' She smiled.

Those days, Vela was thoroughly furious at me. She had found out that Shuchita was meeting me on the sly. Sometimes she cried before me. 'I loved you, but you were never mine.' Vela's behaviour didn't seem like anything more than obstinacy to me. Despite her age, Vela's body was taut. She did not look older than thirty-five. But who would know better the truth behind this appearance than Vela herself? A feeling of vulnerability, and inferiority, kept gnawing at her. She began to behave cruelly with me, even in our intimate moments. On the other hand, Shuchita started yielding herself ever more gratefully. Vela needed me desperately, so she couldn't leave me. At most she could give way to an animal savagery until she finally collapsed from dejection and agitation.

Was I just some object of necessity for Shuchita as well? This thought was like a stab at my heart. Time and again, I tried to console myself, but to no avail. Couldn't Shuchita be mine somehow? But thinking about her policeman-husband, my spirit wavered. Several times, I checked the money in my bank account. In the previous six months, it hadn't gone over two hundred thousand rupees. It had also been six months since Shuchita had come into my life.

'Take me away from here,' she said one day and grabbed my arm. It was as though I had finally been granted my most ardent wish. Varun had gone to Australia for five days. Whatever money I got from Vela, I spent on Shuchita. Just the cost of the hotel room where we were staying was three thousand rupees a night. Shuchita was so honest, she couldn't ask Varun for any money.

It had been raining since morning. Pelting rain. The flower-pots on the balcony had filled to the brim with water. Across the room, through the glass panes, some Arab men were enjoying the rain on a balcony. They had Indian women with them. These desert-dwellers come all the way to Mumbai just to revel in the rain. Every year, the government and the private sector announce special monsoon offers for their customers. Do poor Arabs and Arab women die without ever seeing the rain? Do the poor have caste, religion, or country? Revati was a brahmin, so then why did she die?

Vela was getting jealous. She was getting more emotional. She was also getting older. And fear too was growing in the recesses of her heart. I had neither hatred nor compassion for her. I couldn't think of her as anything more than a regular client. Do shopkeepers get emotionally attached to their customers? But was I a shopkeeper? Was Vela a customer? It seemed to me that we were both merchandise. Or that we were raw material being kicked around between manufacturer, product, and consumer by some invisible trading practice.

'I want to marry Shuchita,' I said as I was cutting the cake Vela brought for me on my twenty-sixth birthday. She had insisted on bringing it. When she heard this, she went quiet for a few moments. 'Bastard!' Vela landed a resounding slap on my ear.

'This won't spoil anything,' I took her hands in mine and held them. She started sobbing like a child. In those tears, for the first time, I saw an innocent Velamma. If she had cried and said, 'I'll die without you', it would not have been difficult for me to figure out that this was all a lie and the tears all a posture. But after she stopped crying, the indistinct words that she coughed up between her hiccups and her tears did not come from Vela's body, but rather from Velamma's heart. 'Why am I grieving over your happiness? This thing is devouring me.' And then she wept for a long time.

Varun was still in Australia. Shuchita stayed with me the whole night. This had been arranged for my birthday. We sat at the Gateway of India late into the night. The stars were faint in the sky. There were many couples there. Were they all broken like us, misfits and useless? We left for the hotel at 2 a.m. Shuchita wrapped herself in silence the whole way. Only I talked a little, now and then. My chatter seemed superficial. Maybe she wasn't listening, maybe I wasn't making any sense. Can a word even be a word without any meaning? They were all as inconsequential as the surf on the ocean shores. Insignificant, indistinguishable, and fleeting. But there is passion in, or born from, those words spoken or written with one's own blood.

'He doesn't need me.' Shuchita placed the bed sheet at her feet and her head at the crown of the bed. 'I'm like a bullet loaded in his gun. He never needs a bullet. Only when they expire does he throw them away.' There was agony in her eyes. Her little face drooped. I was attracted to Shuchita. The size of her face was partly the reason. I found women with small faces charming, like the faces of little children. I imagined taking the faces of such women between my hands and kissing them. This is what I did to Shuchita. The first time I kissed her like that, she cried for a long time. I saw her eyes misting with hope. At daybreak, I dropped her at her house. 'Divorce Varun,' I said on the way.

'He'd rather kill me than divorce me,' she almost screamed, then was quiet for several moments. 'As long as he lives, he won't be able to see me belonging to anyone else. He's just like a wicked child who'd delight in breaking his own toy rather than let another child hold it.'

'What should I do?' Even at that moment my attention turned to my bank balance. This held me back from taking any major step.

'Don't do anything. Finish your studies.' This was clearly meant as a gibe. I had spoken on many occasions of the obstacles to my education. An education that was my goal, my destination, the very breath of my life, for which I had endured everything. The thought of abandoning it grieved me deeply. This was why I latched on to Vela. I didn't speak my heart to anyone besides Shuchita. Before Shuchita, I used to share my thoughts with Sharda. Sharda would dig them out of me. Though Shuchita was at first only a body, at some point she started to mean much more to me. But I could never tell anyone about Vinayak's cruel attack. Whenever I thought about it, a prickling feeling spread across my whole body, as if it were crawling with ants. This was anger, hatred, and fear. How I endured this alone, I don't know.

Varun returned from Australia. Shuchita continued coming as usual. Sometimes Vela's anxiety was quite extreme. She often held my hands and wept. Whenever she cried, I hoped that Velamma would be born from Vela's labour pains, but it seemed like Velamma was inverted in the womb. A breech baby. It put her life at risk. I worried about Velamma. She enjoined me to study. She gave me food on time and remembered to give me a cup of milk before I slept. For the first time in eleven months, she didn't call for me for three weeks. This felt to me like freeloading. Luxurious freeloading.

After being with Shuchita, I didn't even want to touch anyone else. When Vela kissed me, I felt like throwing up. I averted my eyes and spat, or rinsed my mouth. This was completely unexpected. Did Shuchita feel the same way when Varun made love to her, I wondered? I had to do all this, this was my job. Or was this also avarice? Did Shuchita face such a helpless dilemma – between marital obligation and greed? I went on without a word. Can you give your heart to one person and your body to another? Can you physically be with one person and keep thinking of another? Is this a sin? Is it unethical? Could it ever be the case that if you belonged to someone in your heart, you could also be faithful in body to that same person? Could a person's life ever bloom in its own boundless beauty? For all this, you need money, education, and reputation.

'From tomorrow, you get up early and study, and at night, go to bed on time.' These were Vela's words. This was the moment she began to transform into Velamma, like the diaphanous, misty layer between night and daybreak. There wasn't quite a month left before my exams. Twenty-five days had passed, and she hadn't called me to her room.

Father appeared frequently in my dreams: 'You have to study, become a big man. The stream of life flows a long way. You'll forget all this one day; you'll leave it behind.' Sometimes Papa also appeared in a stark white kurta-pyjama with a big turban on his head. I couldn't recognise him. He appeared on the Patel's charpoy, sitting with the Patel, puffing away on the Patel's hookah. And sometimes Baba also appeared: 'Come back now. The Patel's boy is dead. Now you die too.'

Then he beat me with his cane, like he beat his goat. Then I saw myself turning into a goat. I would sit bolt upright, trembling.

Vela had been wronged and had suffered; now Shuchita was feeling anxious, and I ... how had I gotten here? I had not chosen suicide like Revati. We were bound together in this torment. This was our intimate alliance. Then why, instead of understanding each other, did we behave like tyrants? Why weren't we supportive of one another? Had the hatred that led to our suffering settled in our own hearts now? Can't the exquisite catharsis of hatred help us overcome our misery? Or, can't we all become partners in misery? I mulled over this all night long and did not know when I slipped into sleep.

The exams were over. Shuchita phoned almost every day. She bore no malice toward Vela. Vela wasn't angry either when Shuchita called. The evening of my last exam, Vela called me to her room. 'I made one rule in my life, that I would not make any rules. But...but...I've become addicted to you. This body...what can I do?' Her eyes were downcast, her brow too. 'With anyone else...it won't happen again.' Her voice was breaking. It seemed as though she was trying to steel herself, but was thwarted over and over in the attempt. I was silent and inert. 'Oh little child...what can I do?...Didn't Gandhiji call his wife Ba? You know, don't you, Ba means Ma in Gujarati?' She was dealing in hollow arguments to calm her heart. This was playing with fire. She wasn't explaining anything to me, she was consoling herself. I couldn't help her with this. Maybe finally her heart accepted it, or maybe she had killed her heart. I recalled that when a baby is inverted in the womb, chances are either the baby or the mother would die.

Shuchita and I had already decided that we had to be one. No law could help us.

Varun had gone to Nasik for two days. He left in the morning, and Shuchita came to see me in the afternoon. I always saw her arrival as her return – as though she had freed herself from Indra's clutches. I didn't think of this as sin, though not because I questioned the idea of sin. In truth, virtue had died for me, or it had irrevocably changed. This is why repentance never entered my vocabulary. Repentance eclipses a man's strength. That night she stayed with me in the hotel. It was a lovers' night.

Velamma came to me as I was leaving for the hotel. Maybe she knew I was on my way to meet Shuchita. Velamma was dejected. 'Forgive me. I did to you exactly what Deshmukh did to me. We shouldn't be like Deshmukh. We shouldn't force ourselves on anyone. If you're happy, then it ought to make me happy.' I left.

The next day, at 7 a.m., when Shuchita and I were sleeping, there was a knock on the door. I got up to open it, but Shuchita said, 'Wait, I'll go see.' I heard the sound of the door opening. A few moments later, someone in a mask came into my room, but Shuchita was nowhere to be seen.

'Who are you?' There was anger, fear, and surprise in my voice. At that moment, the intruder pulled out a pistol, and before I could say anything else, fired several times. I felt three or four bullets pierce my stomach. As my consciousness wavered, my final thought was: Who is this? Was it Varun…or Vinayak…or Vela? The masked person approached me and kicked me hard in my genitals. I let out a scream at the heart-wrenching pain. The unbearable pain from the kick to my groin was worse than the pain of being shot.

'Okay. Do you know who this is?' A voice reached my consciousness, and I crawled back into the present.

'No,' I screamed. 'Wearing a mask, everyone looks the same. Without a mask, everyone looks different, they are human. You can recognise them.' Spots were dancing in front of my eyes – bright white, and brown like dust. Behind my closed eyes were Baba, Papa, and Father. 'Come back, son, a hungry soul shouldn't eat poison.' I heard Baba's voice. The Patel was smoking Papa's discarded bidi. The villagers had dumped Vinayak, the Patel's son, in the jungle.

'This was a fight…couldn't be concluded…but for Vinayak's crime…can the entire community be punished…would this be justice?…But our caste…why are we lowly? How will our people become strong? Where will we go? What should we do?'

Crime is very seductive. And revenge a trickster.

Afterword: This House of Love

To me, the process of creating literature is like building a house of love that does not have the walls and doors of caste, religion, colour, race and nationality. It's an effort to forge a passport that will make borders and differences disappear. Literature's place must be with the people and their struggles for identity. I cannot think of any other purpose for why I write. The house of literature is not 'a freeloader's den':

कबिरा ये घर प्रेम का, खाला का घर नाहिं
सीस काटि भुंइया धरो, फिर घर पैठो माहिं ॥

This is the house of love, Kabir, not a place where
    freeloaders saunter
Sever your swollen head and fling it aground,
    only then enter

This book is a small effort to build a small house of love. Many friends have helped me; they continue to stand by me, and I hope they will in the future too. My work wouldn't be possible without them.

I would like to thank the various magazines and journals where some of these stories first appeared in Hindi; and the publishers of my books, Arun Maheshwari (Vani Prakashan) and Mahesh Bhardwaj (Samayik Prakashan).

I am grateful to the translator of these stories, my friend Laura Brueck. She recognised the value of my stories, resolved to translate them, and accomplished this task in the midst of raising Hugo. I must apologise to Matt and Hugo, should my stories have denied them some of Laura's attention. However, I do believe Laura must have ably done justice to both responsibilities.

To merely thank my publisher and friend, S. Anand, for his obsession with these stories would be banal. He got me to believe that there was something special and significant about my writing. I salute his passion. Since Anand's frenzy may have hassled her, I must also apologise to his wife, Sivapriya.

I must thank Juli Perczel, who with her good knowledge of Hindi, aided Anand in steering this boat. And indeed, I owe thanks to Raju at Navayana, who became my new reader and was ensnared by Anand into helping him row this boat ashore.

I have not yet had the pleasure of meeting Shyama Haldar, the copyeditor. But her intimate and informed responses to these stories, communicated via Anand, thrilled me.

*I am grateful to Arundhati Roy, author of **The God of Small Things**, who made the time to read my stories and respond to them. She has a unique and extraordinary way of seeing. I am equally indebted to Mohammed Hanif for reading my stories at short notice. I thank him for his generous praise and his faith in my writing.*

I thank my friends Heinz Werner Wessler, Hideaki Ishida, and Alessandra Consolaro who have always encouraged me.

Finally, I am thankful to every member of the 'family of friends', who have chosen to be, and have allowed me to make them, a part of my house of love.

Translator's Note

Ajay Navaria's rich and varied use of language – literary Hindi spliced with English, Rajasthani, and the occasional Punjabi inflection – is what makes his work both exciting and difficult to translate. In an effort to preserve the (seemingly) unmediated experience of reading Navaria's stories in the original, I have avoided footnotes and other marginal explications of certain specific terms, idioms, use of dialects. I have worked instead to preserve the nuance and flavour of Navaria's language in the translation, though as with any translation, there is inevitable loss. One of the defining elements of Navaria's prose, in the original Hindi, is his strategic and self-conscious use of English. Unfortunately, there appeared no straightforward way in which to mark his use of English in the translated versions without distracting unduly from the shape of the stories themselves. I urge anyone who reads these translations, but can also read Hindi, to seek these and his other stories out in Hindi as well.

I want to thank Ajay Navaria for his generous gifts of time, guidance, and engaging and challenging literature that he has shared with me over the years. In the process of translating these stories, I consulted several people, including Ajay, as well as colleagues and friends Rupert Snell, Christi Merrill, and Deepti Misri about how to render particularly challenging elements of dialogue and mood. I have learned a tremendous amount through this collaborative process, and I thank them all.

I am deeply indebted in particular to S. Anand and Juli Perczel, who toiled for long hours to edit, correct, and refine my draft translations; this volume is tremendously improved for their labours and careful attention. I finally want to thank my dear family, in particular Matt and Hugo, for selflessly giving me the time and loving support to complete this book.

AJAY NAVARIA is the author of two collections of short stories, **Patkatha aur Anya Kahaniyan** *(2006) and* **Yes Sir** *(2012), and a novel,* **Udhar ke Log** *(2008). He has been associated with the premier Hindi literary journal,* **Hans**. *He teaches in the Hindi department at Jamia Millia Islamia University in Delhi.*

LAURA BRUECK is Assistant Professor of Hindi literature and South Asian studies at the University of Colorado in Boulder. Her book **Writing Resistance: The Rhetorical Imagination of Hindi Dalit Literature** *was published in 2014 by Columbia University Press.*